THE HAUNTED ASYLUM

BY

ELISA WILKINSON

Published by New Generation Publishing in 2023

First Edition

ISBN: 978-1-80369-830-4

www.newgeneration-publishing.com
New Generation Publishing

INTRODUCTION

Elisa and her husband have lived at their home at Thornes Wakefield for the past sixty three years. She has helped to solve various types of phenomena that people have been experiencing in and outside their homes, she has also solved inexplicable happenings that have occurred in work places such as factories, old mills, farms, and so on.

At times her daughter Lesley Anne has accompanied her, and both have complete faith in what they are doing and are of a Pagan belief. Therefore their trust in spirit guidance, keeps them safe in whatever work they are undertaking.

Elisa`s published books are of true spiritual encounters, and true war stories. She also writes fictional horror stories. She hopes you enjoy reading this book that carries a hint of truth.

The fear of death is man`s worst enemy
It is a fear we cannot see
Unnoticed it walks amongst us
Waiting for you and me

Poem by Elisa Wilkinson

Contents

CHAPTER ONE

RUTH.

Ruth`s heart leapt when hearing the sound of Marks car stopping outside of the secluded cottage that he had bought for them on the North Yorkshire moors. It was their little love nest he had proclaimed his love when he had first brought her there eight months ago

Ruth, peeped around the lace curtain and felt a trickle of excitement run through her as she watched him stroll towards the door then enter the cottage. Within minutes he had taken her in his strapping arms and was holding her close.

"*Oh God how I love him,*" she thought as she ran her fingers through his thick wavy hair, while he kissed her face and neck before releasing her trembling body.

She then watched as he walked over to the chair and removed his jacket to reveal his rugged six feet tall muscular body, before turning his handsome face towards her and looking at her with his deep brown penetrating eyes that melted her very soul. "Mark, I have something to tell you," she began.

"Is there any coffee?" he interrupted, "I could kill a cup my throat`s as dry as snuff.

"Ruth, went into the kitchen and dutifully poured the coffee that she had prepared earlier and placed It on the table beside him. No cream, no milk, no sugar, he liked it black. earlier and placed it on the table beside him. No cream, no milk, no sugar, he liked it black,

"Mark, I must tell you something it is vitally important," she began, stumbling over her words not quite knowing how to explain, then suddenly burst out. "Mark, I`m pregnant."

"What?" he stammered, in amazement almost dropping the cup from his hands.

"Yes, it`s a boy."

Within seconds his handsome features had twisted into an ugly unrecognisable being. "For goodness sake how long have you known?" he snapped moving rapidly across the room before stopping in front of her.

"I`m twelve weeks"

"Shit," he swore, "why the hell didn't you say something before?"

Ruth, stared at him in utter amazement, she hadn't been expecting such a strong negative reaction, she had expected him to be pleased at the thoughts of them having a child together, especially a son.

"You`ve got to get rid of it," he stipulated instantly, infuriated at the idea of becoming trapped in a loveless triangle, Mark, enjoyed playing the field, and with his looks he had the choice of any woman he wanted. No, he was determined to stay a free man and do as he liked and not be tied down to a submissive woman and a squalling brat. "I will pay for the abortion, I know a clinic that will keep it quiet, nobody will know who you are," he said taking his mobile phone out and began dialling.

Ruth, cringed at the icy tone in his voice and dropped onto the sofa stunned with shock. She couldn't believe what she was hearing, the man who had professed his deep undying love for her was now on his mobile phone arranging an abortion for her. "No" she yelled jumping to her feet, "I am not going to murder my unborn child." She screamed at him, pummelling him with her fists.

"Shut up, you, stupid bitch," he snapped.

Turning towards her, he slapped her face and pushed her down onto the sofa. "You will do as I say."

Tears, streamed down her face as she heard him arranging the abortion, then clicked off his phone and glared at her with a look of pure hatred in his eyes.

Her voice was barely audible as she stammered through her distressing sobs. "Mark, please don't do this to me, not to us, not to our baby."

"Forget about the fucking baby, it's already history," he snarled.

"Mark," she began pleading.

"I said forget it, and I'm not marrying you."

"But Mark, you promised."

"I said a lot of things to get between your legs, I was on the understanding that you were taking birth control tablets, so what happened there?" He snarled, pushing his face up to hers so that she could feel his hot breath on her face. "I never expected you to get pregnant and you're not trapping me with that old trick," he declared in a cold heartless voice.

"I can tell you now, there has been plenty more where you came from and there's plenty more willing to take your place, so you can pack your bags and get out. Friday at three I will pick you up and take you to the clinic, understand?" he growled, glaring at her.

Ruth stared at him, in disbelief at what was happening one day they were the perfect couple and the next this total catastrophe. "Oh God," she sobbed, burying her face in her hands. "I can't believe this is happening," she cried. "Mark please won't you reconsider?"

"Listen to me," he shouted. "I can't marry you and I don't want to, I'm already married and have three kids that I can't stand, and I don't want any more brats round my neck, do you understand?" He snarled taking her by the shoulders and shaking her. "You stupid cow, you've ruined everything, we had a good thing going until this."

He stopped speaking for a moment, as he stared down at her with hate filled eyes, for a few seconds Ruth felt a twinge of fear run through her. Nobody knew she was living at the lonely cottage in the middle of nowhere, there was no passing traffic only the odd hitchhiker who gave the cottage a wide berth. And now in this uncontrollable fit of temper, it looked as if he was about to kill her.

"Mark you're hurting me let go of me," she cried, when feeling the strong pressure of his fingers pressing into the soft muscle of her throat.

Mark hesitated and for a brief moment, as a look of realization spread across his face at what he was about to do. He released his grip on her throat and pushed her down onto the sofa then strode over to the chair to pick up his jacket, then walked to the door and turned. "Remember," he growled in a threatening tone. "I will pick you up Friday at three, and have your bags packed you're moving out."

Ruth stared after him in disbelief, unable to understand what was happening. She had mistakenly believed that he would have been overjoyed at the thought of a baby especially a boy. She watched as he marched sullenly to the door, and without a backward glance, he opened it, then slammed it shut as he walked away, out of her life.

CHAPTER TWO,

SUICIDE.

The following morning, when Ruth, arrived at work, she was met at the door by the arrogant, condescending Matron in charge of the unit. "What`s the matter with you?" she asked, when seeing the dark circles beneath Ruth`s red rimmed eyes.

"Nothing`s the matter," Ruth, replied, then ran to the washroom to throw up. "You've been doing that every morning for the past four weeks," she said when Ruth, Returned, ashen faced to her locker and began putting her uniform on.

I would like to bet you`re pregnant?" the Matron commented in an obnoxious tone. "It`s nothing to do with you," Ruth, replied tartly, wishing the woman would just fade away and die Somewhere, where no one would ever find her.

"You can`t hide it from me young lady, then on second thoughts, I can`t call you a lady in your condition can I?" she scoffed maliciously. And I can guess who the father is, don`t think I haven't seen you two together in Mark Armstrong`s Jaguar car."

Ruth, stared at her in stunned surprise. "*how did she know who she was meeting.*" Both herself and Mark thought they were being discreet only meeting in secluded areas and at the cottage.

"Has he told you to have an abortion like he did the others?" she added with a sly grin. "What others?" Ruth, felt her jaw drop open in surprise.

"It`s alright, he does it with them all when they drop pregnant."

"What do you mean with them all? And what others? What are you talking about?" Ruth`s voice quivered as she spoke.

"Oh I know most of the sleezy things that Mark gets up to, you see he`s my brother, he tells me about everything that he does with women, he enjoys bragging about his conquests.

"You mean------"

"He holds nothing back," the Matron sniggered, causing the fat to wobble beneath her chin as she chortled maliciously.

In fact he laughed when telling me how easy it was to fuck you in the back seat of his car, or in a field anywhere he could, he enjoyed getting his rocks off." She grinned, relishing in watching the young woman squirm. Ruth, could hardly believe what she was hearing. He`s five years older than me, he arranged for my abortion when I was thirteen years old," she continued giving a sanctimonious grin.

Ruth`s hand flew to her mouth in horror. "You don`t mean-----"Yes I do, he can be very persuasive when he wants to be can`t he? "Ruth, felt sick to her stomach when the realization hit her of what the woman was hinting and of what Mark, truly was. "Oh my God," she gasped. In a moment of panic, Ruth, felt that she had to get away from the woman and all of the disgusting things she was saying.

Frustrated and unable to accept the truth of what Mark, really was, Ruth, raced blindly away from the building, not knowing where she was going. Until she was forced to stop running when finding herself thoroughly winded and unable to draw her breath.

She then felt herself wondering about the baby and leant against the stone wall of the railway bridge for support.

"Would her unborn child a boy be a serial sex offender like his father or would he be a normal little boy?"

"I can`t take that chance!" she cried at the violation of her love for a man who was nothing more than a pervert, who targeted and coveted young women for his sexual perverted lust. Within minutes, Ruth, had made her decision, she felt her heart breaking as she climbed onto the parapet of the old railway bridge and waited for a few moments until hearing the vibrating sound of the hooting engine as it thundered closer, then threw herself down onto the electrified track in front of the oncoming Express train.

CHAPTER THREE,

PSYCHIC INVESTIGATORS

"Good grief I can hardly see where I`m driving," Joan, grumbled as she strove to see through the windscreen of her car. The dense fog that was now swirling across the vast North Yorkshire Moors, spun eerily about the car, and was becoming thicker by the minute.

The sat-nav had taken her away from the A65 Ilkley`s main road and she was now driving along a narrow bumpy lane on the moors towards Hollow Moor. This led to the Moorland Grange, that had been built many years ago away from the main road, that had now become a hospital for the mentally ill.

"Mum,"

"What?"

"Who, or what, do you think is causing the hauntings at the hospital?" Her daughter Anne, asked, who was sat grinding her teeth as she stared anxiously into the mist, trying to see where they were heading.

"I believe," Joan, said to her daughter, trying to break the tension of the hazardous conditions surrounding them, "that there are a number of reasons for the property being haunted especially when you consider the age of the building and it`s past history."

Puzzled Anne looked at her mum "What do you mean about its past history and age? "Joan began to explain.

"It was first a private residence built in the seventeenth century by a wealthy land owner who lost his fortune due to his, and his sons gambling debts. He shot all three of them before turning the gun on himself and his wife. Then there were other owners who lost the property through similar circumstances. It is said that over the years, most of the land had been sold to pay off the owner`s debts, and that only a few acres were left along with the mansion. However, the many families who had purchased the property, hastily departed due to the ghost sightings and the weird phenomena taking place in the manor, also the inexplicable number of deaths taking place there." "In time, it became derelict because of its sinister reputation and was finally purchased by the North Yorkshire Authority, Where it became a lunatic asylum, then a hospital for the wounded soldiers in the 1st WW. It was later turned into a museum, before becoming a hospital again for the wounded, shell shocked, and dying service men during the 2nd WW."

"Afterwards it became an asylum for the people who were declared to be uncontrollable and needed to be locked away from the public."

"Oh how sad," Anne remarked softly, " the poor souls." Anyway, Joan carried on explaining. "The only sensible stipulation made by the owners was, that before the Grange was demolished, the ground floor must remain open for problem patients only, along with the nurses` quarters, the staff canteen, and patient facilities. However the remaining unused sections of the building were now locked, and had been declared unsafe for anyone to enter.

The plans were that after the patients had been found beds in other hospitals, then Moorland Grange would be demolished to make way for a new private paying hospital that was to be built in its place. In the meantime all of the out buildings and old stables had been demolished and the ground where they once stood had been levelled out and prepared for the new building project."

CHAPTER FOUR

GHOST SIGHTINGS

Although it was only three thirty, due to the dense swirling fog and the thick blanket of falling snow, the daylight was swiftly disappearing so quickly that the overcast sky gave the appearance of approaching nightfall. Combined by the buildings ancient blackened structure, the first view of the Grange gave an austere and malevolent appearance. As its towering medieval chimneys soared high into the dark skyline that were now steadily disappearing beneath a thick blanket of snow and fog.

"Isn`t it stunning?" Joan announced giving a gasp of admiration as she drew the car to a halt in front of the impressive building. "It`s beautiful," she almost purred, the four Corinthian column`s supporting the wrought iron balcony spanning the complete front of the second story of the building`s facia, stretched from one end of the building to the other. The leaded light windows on either side of the entrance were about twelve feet in height by six feet wide, with a central dividing stone pillar separating the windows on either side.

Anne was also staring at the building, but found herself wondering why there were iron bars fitted at every window on the three story building. But before she could ask, Joan, was already pointing out that they had been placed there for the patient`s own safety.

As in some cases, the patients were liable to open the patio doors and leap from the balcony after watching the birds flying overhead when believing they could fly like the birds. But after leaping from the great height they were either killed or badly injured from the fall.

They did notice though, that the only part of the Grange in use, was the ground floor while the upper two stories were in complete darkness. The only visible course of light that at times filtered through the swirling mist and falling snow came from the light shining from the hallway's glass panels in the door that led into the hospital.

Joan, who stood five feet two inches tall, was of a slim build with long black and grey speckled hair and was a registered professional paranormal expert. She had been contacted and invited by the panel of trustees to investigate the haunting at the asylum. She was asked to film the apparitions whenever possible, then to report her findings back to them.

However within minutes of their arrival at the Grange, Joan, felt her body tense when feeling herself drawn to look up towards the first floor window.

Through the swirling patches of fog and snow, she caught sight of the illuminated, ghostly apparition, of a thin, pale faced woman peering down at her from the upstairs window of the derelict area above. Within seconds of being noticed, the woman had vanished from sight.

"Did you see that?" Joan, gasped, turning towards her daughter Anne, who often accompanied her on the investigations.

Anne, who was sat motionless staring at the window responded, "Yes I did. Didn't they say that it was only the patient's and nurse's quarters that were haunted? If so, then I think somebody got that wrong don't you?"

"Yes," her mum replied. "I believe there's more going on here than what I was informed of, and I think it is going to take more than the five days we were given, to sort this little problem out."

"Yes and I hope there's some lighting in the areas where we're going?" Anne mumbled, "and some heating," she added, shuddering at the thought of it being cold.

"In parts there are, but in others, no there isn't." Joan answered, "all of the amenities in the unused part of the hospital have been turned off, only the wards for the patients on the ground floor, and the nurse quarters along with the canteen and patient facilities still have the necessary services."

"That's all we need," Anne, moaned, being able to see where we're going and freezing to death."

"Stop griping," her mum snapped angrily. "You practically begged to join me on this investigation, it's too late now to start complaining, so shut up."

Anne pulled a face and dropped silent, not wanting to stretch her mother's patience, and for a while they sat quietly, as their eyes searched the building for any more signs of activity. But when nothing else occurred, Joan decided to unload their luggage from the vehicle and get into the hospital where they would be much warmer and safer.

She hoped.

CHAPTER FIVE

THE STRANGER

"Let's get the baggage and equipment out of the back of the car then we can go to our room and get warm." Joan urged, opening the car door and letting in a draft of cold air.

"For goodness' sake mum, do you have to open the door so wide? You're letting all of the heat out of the car," Anne whinged when feeling the cold rush of air penetrate her body.

"Stop moaning and get yourself moving, and help me with these bags. That way you will keep warm."

Anne gave a sigh of resignation she fastened her coat and pulled the thick. woolly hat over her head, then the furry sheepskin gloves over her dithering hands, before clambering out of the warmth of the four by four SUV and dropped into the deep snow.

Within seconds of her feet hitting the ground she felt herself sinking up to her ankles in the slush and snow, and grabbed hold of the door handle when feeling her feet sliding away from beneath her.

"Oh shit," she yelled. "Mother!"

"What's wrong now?" she heard her mum call impatiently.

"Nothing," Anne replied, pulling herself upright and hardly daring to move as the snow and ice cold wind whipped around her.

`Bugger this,` she muttered to herself and made a move to climb back into the car, then froze when hearing her mum's angry voice.

"Get back here, immediately.

"Anne cringed, then muttering silent curses she turned slowly, and hanging onto the saturated side of the vehicle, she began making her way towards the rear. Then let out a cry of frustration when feeling her feet sliding from beneath her and landed flat on her back, with a thud that knocked the breath out of her.

"Get up you idiot," Joan snapped glaring down at her, as she lifted the last of the luggage from the car and slammed the tailgate down, then locked the vehicle. "Stop messing about and bring those two bags," she instructed pointing to the last two bags that were quickly becoming covered with snow.

Joan herself had to struggle to stay upright, she picked up as much baggage as she could carry and made her way towards the vestibule leaving Anne alone to wrestle herself to her feet.

"Mum! Don`t leave me!" she cried, but her words were lost when they were carried away by the roaring wind. At that moment, Anne, felt a surge of panic sweep through her, as she watched her mother disappear into the swirling clouds of fog and snow. She struggled against the cumbersome weight of her thick clothing while attempting to regain her footing. But being only short and chunky, she was unable to reach anything to pull herself upright and could feel the cold wet snow beginning to soak into her jeans. Not only that, but the snow was falling directly into her face and blurring her vision.

"Oh hell," she cursed, when feeling her feet sliding every time she attempted to raise herself. "This isn't going to do my hem-aroids any good` she grimaced and grabbed hold of the wet tyre in an effort to pull herself to her feet, then felt a pang of alarm when hearing a man`s voice speaking in an amused tone.

"Can I be of any assistance?" he asked extending his hand towards her.

Anne rubbed the snow from her eyes so she could see more clearly who was speaking, and looked up to find a handsome middle aged man gazing down at her with a smile of amusement on his face, as she lay struggling in the cold, wet slush trying desperately to get to her feet.

"Oh cripes!" she moaned, when realising the vulnerable situation she was in. "No thanks, I`m alright, she replied as pleasantly as she could, flushing with embarrassment. "I can manage on my own." Yet inwardly thinking `what a time to show myself up!`

"As you prefer" he replied. She noticed a flicker of amusement cross his pleasant features, and watched as he slipped his gloved hands into to his pockets and walked away, disappearing into the fog.

`Awe shit, why did I have to sound so rude?` she chided herself, `he was only trying to be helpful.

Then supressed a cry of alarm, when seeing that there was no sign of his footprints in the deep snow where he had just walked by.

"Awe bugger," she cursed, "I`ve just seen a ghost!"

Within seconds, Anne was on her feet, and with no sign of Joan, the realisation that she was alone with a ghost wandering about the hospital grounds filled her with untold terror.

Then, when an sharp gust of cold air swept past her, Anne screamed with fright, she snatched up the two remaining cases, and raced towards the elusive spot of light emanating from the building`s windows, that appeared and disappeared as the grey mist floated aimlessly about them.

"Mother where are you?" she called frantically, keeping her voice low, while at the same time trying not to let her fear get the better of her, then gave a gasp of relief when seeing her mum through the swirling fog standing in the partially lit foyer ringing the door-bell waiting to gain entrance into the hospital.

"Mum, you`re never going to believe what`s just happened?" she began.

Then shrank back in fear when the woman turned towards her.

"Oh my God" Anne groaned, when seeing a look of insanity plastered across the face of a toothless grinning old woman staring back at her.

"Anne? Anne? Are you alright?" she heard her mother's voice, and stared at her through a trembling haze of fear and unease.

"Where did she go?"

"Who? What are you talking about?"

"That woman, she was standing next to you," Anne replied shakily. "There's no one here but me," her mother answered giving a her a look of concern. "Why doesn't someone answer the bloody door before we freeze to death?" Joan snapped irritably rattling the door handle.

"Mum, mum, please listen to me for a moment will you?" Anne pleaded grabbing hold of her mother's arm as she tried to explain what had happened.

Just then the figure of a stout woman dressed in a Matron's uniform appeared in the brightly lit hallway. "Shush" her mother chided, "be quiet, and let me do the talking,"

CHAPTER SIX

THE MATRON

Anne dropped quiet as they waited for the door to be opened, but they never expected it to be answered by a grim faced, stocky, middle aged demanding woman. "Who are you? What do you want?" she enquired sharply. "Whatever you are selling we are not buying," she snapped, glancing down at their luggage and made as if to close the door.

Immediately Joan's hackles shot up by the woman's ignominious attitude. "We are here under the instructions of the Board of Trustees to find out what is causing the disruptions in this hospital," Joan informed the woman.

"I am Joan Shepherd and this is my daughter Anne, now if you don't mind, I would appreciate if you would allow us inside out of the cold, and for you to show us to the quarters that have been allocated to us?"

From the dour grimace of resignation on the woman's face, Joan didn't need to say any more. The woman opened the door wider and stepped to one side, allowing them to enter, then as soon as they were inside, she slammed the door shut and locked it.

"I am Patrice Ellison the Matron of this hospital, she curtly introduced herself. You can move freely about the designated areas of the hospital, but if you wish to go into the areas that are considered off limits, then you must first have permission from me. I don't want you pestering any of my patients and members of staff with unnecessary questions. Do I make myself clear."

"Yes you have made yourself quite clear," Joan replied through gritted teeth, not wanting to add fuel to the fire by responding as she normally would have done, and was shocked by the Matron`s haughty, self-centred attitude.

"Good, so long as you understand, I will now show you to your quarters. When you have made yourselves comfortable, you can go into the staff canteen where warm refreshments can be acquired, you will have to pay for them of course."

Joan cringed when Anne mimicked. "Of course we will have to pay, everything has its price."

The Matron threw Anne a withering look that would have brought a grown man to his knees. But Anne being the person she was, just smiled graciously and followed the Matron along a wide, white, tiled corridor until reaching a wide, mahogany door, that she unlocked and led them into a high ceilinged, spacious room.

They were surprised to find it warm and comfortably furnished with a table and four chairs, plus two easy chairs. There was a wall cupboard containing different beverages and drinking utensils, below that, was a compact area for making tea or coffee and a kettle was provided. While beneath the unit was a small fridge, in the drawers were hand towels and tea towels, while in the cupboard there were cleaning utensils.

One door in the room led into a bedroom containing two single beds, two wardrobes and two chests of drawers and a bedside lamp beside each bed. In the bedroom to the right, another door led into a small, but compact bathroom, containing a bath, shower, sink, and toilet, and a cupboard, where bath towels and soap were stored.

It was obvious that it was used as a room for the night nurse`s comfort. The Matron however, gave them a hostile glare, then without another word she threw the key to the room down onto the table, and watched as it slid across the polished wood and clattered onto the floor, then with a sanctimonious glance, she left the room, slamming the door loudly behind her.

"What the Dickins was that all about?" Joan, declared loudly, at the same bristling with anger at the Matron`s offensive attitude.

"I don`t know and I don`t care," Anne, thundered, "all I can say is thank goodness she`s gone, the old bag was really starting to rattle my cage."

"Mine as well," Joan replied as she removed her wet clothing, then flopped down into one of the well-worn but comfortable armchairs. "She was beginning to push my patience, what do you want to do? Eat first or unpack?"

"I think I should change my clothes first, then we can eat," Anne replied. "My pants are soaking wet after falling in the snow."

Annes removed her boots and wet clothing before changing into a dry pair of pants and slid her feet into a comfortable pair of shoes, then went into the bathroom to scrub her face and hands and comb her hair. "Do you think we are presentable enough for that old ….."

"Anne" her mother chided, "come on, and be on your best behaviour," she warned, as she opened the door and stepped out into the corridor. They followed the sign pointing towards the canteen then stopped short when they stepped inside.

"Oh my God" Anne, groaned when glancing about the canteen and observing the dismal state it was in. "Are we expected to eat in here?"

"Just be thankful we are getting something warm to eat," Joan, whispered when the groups of nurses seated at the tables noticed them, and stopped talking to stare at the newcomers.

Joan, however, moved forward unfazed by the strange looks they were being given, to introduced herself and Anne, and was surprised when she discovered that they were expecting her, and most of them welcomed her with open arms.

By now, Anne, was starving and glanced about the eatery searching for a table that had been cleared, before finally settling at one near the buffet counter. She had noticed though, that the wooden tables and chairs appeared to date back to the late nineteen eighties.

The self- service heated counter where the food was kept warm under huge lights seamed to be from a later period, and the dented metal tea urn that looked as if it had seen better days appeared to have been purchased from a second hand shop.

Thankfully the mismatched mugs and dishes weren't chipped and the cutlery was straight and clean.

Regardless of what the surroundings looked like, Anne`s, stomach rumbled when she smelt the food, `*to blazes with it*, `she thought, `*I`m hungry,*` and gave Joan, a nudge. "What do you say mum, shall we or shan`t we?"

Joan, gave her a wicked grin, "Let`s tuck in, after all we are paying for it aren`t we?"

Within minutes they had each picked up a plate and heaped on a pile of chicken stew and vegetables before re-seating themselves and began eagerly tucking into their meal.

"Anne."

Anne, looked up. "What."

"Why were you screaming when I left you by the car to bring in the two bags of luggage?"

"Oh, you are not going to believe this," Anne, mumbled through a mouthful of food. She went on to explain about the man who had offered to help her when she had fallen, and hadn't realised that he was a ghost, until he had walked away leaving no footprints in the deep snow.

"What?" Joan almost shouted. "Why didn't you say something before?" she hissed when noticing the strange looks passing between some of the nurses who were staring at them.

"Because you wouldn't listen."

"Well I`m listening now, did he speak to you?"

"Yes, he asked if I needed any help."

"What did you say?"

"I told him I was alright I could manage."

"Where did he go?"

"He actually walked straight through you and the door when you were trying to get into the hospital, then there was that horrible old woman who was stood beside you, who vanished as soon as the door was opened."

"Bloody Hell Anne, why didn't you tell me sooner?"

"I tried to, but you wouldn't listen, by then you were too busy arguing with that silly, fat bitch."

"Oh for goodness` sake" Joan, groaned, rubbing her head in frustration.

"It`s not my fault, you wouldn't listen." Anne, complained. "You never do."

CHAPTER SEVEN

THE MATRONS WARNING.

The following morning just after finishing breakfast, the Matron appeared at the canteen door and approached them.

"Might I have a word with you two?" she asked, "It won`t take long what I have to say."

"Yes, sit down," Joan, replied, indicating towards an empty chair.

"No thank you," she replied haughtily, "I prefer to stand."

With the look on the Matrons face they immediately knew it was trouble. The Matron stood squarely beside them with a harsh look on her face before speaking clearly and loudly enough for everyone in the dining hall to hear her. "I do not approve of what you are about to do, in fact if it was up to me you wouldn`t be here at all." she spat in an acidic tone.

"Well it isn`t up to you is it?" Anne, broke in, then looked at Joan and felt herself wilt when her mother`s irritable glare told her to shut up.

Joan. rose to her feet to face the Matron on equal terms.

"First of all" she began in a scathing tone, "It was the Board of Governors who approached me to ask if I would investigate the strange goings on at this hospital." "Secondly you are well aware that they wanted a complete investigation as to what could be causing the amount of psychic activity that is occurring here." "Thirdly they want to know why the nurses were leaving or threatening to leave. And finally there has been a large number of patient and staff suicides reported, therefore permission was granted for me to carry out my investigations." "Now if you don't mind, I would like to finish my meal in peace before I start an inspection of the wards that are affected by the phenomena," Joan added waving her hand in a dismissive gesture.

The silence in the canteen was deafening until a number of nurses who didn't want to be caught up in the crossfire hastily departed.

Fuming the Matron informed Joan, and Anne, that she would not be accompanying them, nor would she be responsible for any mishaps that may occur while they were investigating any part of the hospital. She then pushed a diagram towards them with areas that she had ringed showing a number of completely different regions that were affected by the phenomenon, from where they had been asked to investigate.

Puzzled, Joan, studied the diagram for a few minutes before asking why she had not been informed of any other part of the hospital being haunted. Especially the areas that the Matron had indicated on the map that was supporting the theory that highly active phenomenon was taking place. "Why wasn't I informed about this?" Joan, stared hard at the Matron angrily. A smirk touched the corner of the Matron's mouth, then subsequently she removed a key from her pocket and placed it onto the table in front of Joan. Joan, could feel the resentment rising inside of her, at the Matron's unpleasant attitude. "What is that for?" she asked, fighting to control her temper.

"We always keep that door locked," the Matron remarked spitefully, pointing towards a door that was partially concealed by a screen. "The only access to the unoccupied vicinity of the hospital is through that door, therefore whenever you leave this room, I must insist that you lock the door immediately you are through. Have I made myself clear?" she announced sharply.

"Oh no, not again," Anne, mumbled.

Quite clear," Joan replied. "But why must the door be kept locked?" she enquired, trying to appear unruffled by the sanctimonious bitch who was beginning to get under her skin.

"Because we don`t know who, or what, is lingering about in the corridor behind that door, and we don't want whatever it is coming in here and disturbing the nurses any more than is necessary," the Matron responded. "That door is your only means of escape from whatever is lurking in that corridor so don't lose the key, otherwise?" The look in her steel hard grey eyes spoke a million words, and from the look alone on the Matron`s face she didn't need to say anymore.

Joan felt a sense of unease as she picked up the key from the table and slid it into her Pocket. She did however, notice the Matrons strange look of concern before turning away leaving them both staring after her departing figure. "Don't forget what I told you," she said when reaching the open door. "Keep that door locked as soon as you get into the corridor, and don`t let anyone else go through there with you. No-one but yourselves must enter that corridor. The Matron then left slamming the dining hall door loudly behind her.

"Well you certainly put the old wind bag in her place," one of the nurses called from across the canteen.

"Yes and you made your point clear enough." another nurse expressed, "but I must warn you, take extreme care when you go through that door," the nurse pointed to the door behind the screen. She then settled back in her seat and began speaking in a low tone to the other nurses, who gave Joan, and Anne, a worried glance before, they carried on whispering amongst themselves.

"Well what did you think to that?" Anne, asked, wondering why the matron was making such a big deal about keeping the door locked.

"Goodness only knows," Joan, replied, getting to her feet and scooping up the empty dishes. "But I suppose we had better do as she asks or else," she grinned when drawing her hand across her throat.

"Yes boss" Anne, replied with a giggle, "anything you say boss."

"Cheeky!" Joan, remarked giving her a motherly slap on the head.

"Come on, let`s take these plates back to the counter, then we can go to our room and make our plans for an early start in the morning. But first we need to take a look around the four wards tonight while the patients are sleeping, otherwise they may become disturbed when seeing strangers wandering about the wards.

CHAPTER EIGHT

INCIDENT ON THE WOMENS WARD

Joan, had been warned by the Matron, and Sister Andrews, who was in charge of the four wards during the night, that it would be best for the patients if she were to wait until eleven pm to carry out her investigation, by then, all of the patients would be sedated and sleeping. Joan, agreed with their suggestion. Sister Andrews, also insisted that they conduct their inquiries as quietly as possible, so as not to disturb the patients."

"We won`t be doing anything tonight," Joan, informed her. "We only want to take a look around each ward this evening before deciding what equipment we will be needing for the investigation tomorrow night."

That`s fine, sister Andrews, replied.

"Where are the rest of the occupants?" Joan, asked, when noticing that the ward was almost empty. " I was informed there were twelve patients, one to each bed.

"There are, but the ones who are capable of interaction are in the Recreation Room."

"Where is that? And what do they do there?" Anne, raised the question before her mother had the opportunity to do so.

Sister Andrews, was surprised by Annes, outspoken query. "Every afternoon, both male and female patients are taken to the Recreation Room where they are allowed to mix for a short period of time. That is where they play simple board games, and cards, etc. The patients are watched over by two male and four female nurses, who encourage the patients to use whatever mental capabilities they are capable of using."

"Afterwards they are served their evening meal in an adjoining room before being brought back to the ward, where they are bathed and given their medication before bedding down."

In an unforeseen move, the sister unexpectedly took hold of Joan`s arm and guided her to the farthest point of the ward, away from the four remaining bed` ridden patients who were propped up in their beds watching them. "I would like to have a word with you in private," she whispered, glancing furtively about the ward. "There is something you must be made aware of, it`s about the hauntings. I really shouldn't be telling you this, but on a number of occasions the patients on all four wards have seen something that has panicked them. This has caused mayhem on the wards and it has taken ages for the nurses to calm them down, but as you can expect, when one start`s screaming they all follow suit. Even some of the nurses have seen things they are afraid to speak about."

She was about to say more when one of the nurses popped her head around the door.

"I will have to bring Ivy, back to the ward," she announced, rolling her eyes and glancing towards Joan, before passing her a warm smile. "She has had a little accident and needs bathing."

"Sister Andrews, quickly regained her composure. "I will have the bathroom prepared." She picked up the phone on her desk and began dialling. "Nurse Thomson, could you please come to Ward One immediately? there is a patient in need of attention?"

She replaced the telephone, just as a young nurse pushed Ivy, through in her wheelchair.

"I`m afraid she`s in a bit of a mess," the nurse began, before Ivy, started screaming.

"Don`t leave me in there on my own!" she yelled, pointing a long bony finger towards the bathroom. "She`s in there, I know, I`ve just seen her go in."

"What are you talking about Ivy?" the nurse spoke calmly. "There`s no one in the bathroom."

"There is, I`ve just watched her go through that wall over there," Ivy pointed a trembling finger towards the wall.

"What did she look like?" Joan, asked, taking hold of Ivy`s hand. Ivy, stared at her for a moment. "I don`t know you, are you new here?"

"Yes I am," Joan, replied` I have come to help."

"Good they need somebody who knows what they are doing round here," she mumbled, throwing a contemptuous look towards the Sister. "They think I`m bloody daft, but I`m not you know. It`s this lot here, none of these silly buggers knows what they`re doing."

Sister Andrews gave a sigh of exasperation, she was relieved however, to notice the calming effect Joan, was having on Ivy. I`ll tell you what Ivy, I will go into the bathroom first to make sure nobody is in there, then it will be just you the nurse and me. How does that suit you?"

Ivy, gave a toothless grin. "I had to eat my supper without my teeth," she giggled, as saliva ran down her chin. "I forgot to put them in, it's a good thing it was soup and a sandwich. I dipped the sandwich in my soup so I could chew it." she commented, giving a mischievous chortle as she spoke.

"Come on Ivy, let`s get you undressed and into the bath, then you will be comfortable and ready for bed." The nurse gave Ivy, a gentle nudge, before pushing the wheelchair into the bathroom.

Joan, entered first, then turned to Ivy, telling her that it was safe to enter, whereupon Ivy, was happy to allow the nurse to wheel her inside to bath her.

Joan, however was deeply perturbed when she returned to sister Andrews. "Before you say anything, I have noticed the apparition of a beautiful young nurse moving slowly from bed to bed. She then whispers something to each patient as she is stroking their heads, and whatever she is saying it appears to calm them down. In my opinion, I believe that some of the nurses have also seen her." Joan, watched as the sister's features alternated between the truth and what she was afraid to admit.

"Oh my God," she whispered fearfully, as her eyes frantically searched every inch of the ward. "I've never seen her, but I have heard the rumours. Now if you will excuse me," Sister Andrews hurried away, calling for Nurse Davis, to come and keep an eye on the patients.

CHAPTER NINE

ORIGINAL PLANS OF THE GRANGE

The following morning after breakfast, Joan and Anne returned to their room to study the plans given to Joan by the Trust, also the diagram sketched by the Matron.

The entrance to the Grange Hospital Sanitorium was of a grand scale, On the ground level to the right, were four wards` two Women`s at the front of the building and two Men`s behind, and dividing the wards were long corridors. Each ward contained a bathroom, two baths, two showers, and two handbasins` the four toilets were separated for privacy into small cubicles without doors.

To the left at the front of the building was the nurse`s quarters, and to the rear, the staff dining hall and kitchens. Behind the dining hall was the patient`s small recreation room. These rooms were separated by long dimly lit corridors, and the door concealed behind the screen in the dining hall, led onto the corridor that was forbidden for anyone to enter.

Joan had been puzzled when the Matron handed her the key to investigate what lay behind the locked door` she had been led to believe that it was only the patients` quarters that she would be investigating.

Regardless, of what was concerning her, Joan, recalled that because she had been extremely cold when they reached the hospital, she had not taken any notice of the door leading into the entrance. But on the plans, it showed a wide, solid oak door, with a huge crescent moon, leaded light, stained glass window above, while on either side of the door were two arched, stained glass windows, approximately two feet wide by four feet high.

Sadly though, on inspection every window now was cracked and barred. Leading from the door, the plan showed a spectacular fifteen feet wide, mahogany carved Staircase, centrally placed in a spacious, wide open area. At some time, this had been closed off by a long, high, plywood structure with a locked door in its centre` this barricade spanned out into the corridor leading to the rear of the building. There was a door set in one the sides, leading into what was the patients` recreation room behind the staff canteen.

Beside the main central staircase leading up onto a balcony on the first floor, was an old antiquated lift, that consisted of brass concertina gates, and this appeared to have been there ever since the property was first built. At the head of the staircase, was a balcony that spanned the entire floor connecting each of the spacious rooms on either side. Each room was divided by a long corridor.

From there, a second mahogany staircase led onto the second floor, that carried a balcony identical to the one on the first floor that surrounded the entire building. When it reached the farthest point of the building towards the left, It then spiralled upwards until reaching the attic balcony, this was only approachable by a much narrower staircase.

It showed on the map of the Manor, there were two balconies that encircled its entire length, from where a number of rooms and long corridors led to various areas of the building. On looking upwards, it clearly showed on the map that the centre space was a vast open area, also every room on both upstairs floors was separated by long dark corridors.

Additionally, It showed a narrow staircase at the furthermost point at the rear of the building, with a door on the ground floor, that led directly onto the balcony of each floor, and this would have been used by the servant`s.

CHAPTER TEN

START OF THE INVESTIGATION

After breakfast, by eight thirty, Joan and Anne made the decision to first investigate the upper floors of the hospital, the problem was however, that the only way to get there was through the door in the dining hall. On the map the matron had given Joan, it showed there was a servants' staircase leading onto the first balcony, which they decided to use to gain access to the upper floors.

They dressed in warm outdoor clothing, as there was no heating in the part of the abandoned section of the building where they were going, therefore they knew it would be cold and damp.

Each carried a camcorder and had a portable infra-red head torch with camera strapped to their heads. This left them hands' free to record any specific events that their headsets may not pick up, while they were inside searching that area of the property.

They also had a belt strapped around the waists of their multi pocketed pants, that held various pieces of equipment that would be needed in the investigation, along with a knife, bottled water and sandwiches in case of an emergency.

The only problem now, was that the one way to enter the corridor was through the door in the dining hall where Joan, hoped they wouldn't come across the interfering Matron. Thankfully, the only people they met in the dining hall were the nursing staff and two medics, who wished them good luck and informed Joan, that the Matron was busy elsewhere in the hospital.

The staff then watched in nervous anticipation, as Joan, took the key from her pocket to unlock the restricted door and pushed it open, then entered the corridor with Anne.

Subsequently she turned and locked the door securely behind her and was shocked to instantaneously feel a mass of sticky, fine tissue cover her face, and creeping entities crawling all over head and body.

"Mum, I can`t see anything and somethings touching my head!" Anne yelled loudly. "I know and something is crawling all over my hands and face!" Joan yelled frantically brushing aside the substance clinging to her head.

Without further ado, Joan switched on her head lamp and saw that they were immersed in cobwebs, filth and grime. Giant spiders with swollen bodies that were unaccustomed to the bright light, scuttled across their webs in an attempt to escape from the intruders, who had invaded their coveted domain.

But as they struggled to dash the spiders from their clothing, which was practically an impossibility, they found they were sending up thick clouds of choking dust from the floor, as they struggled to brush the crawling creatures away from themselves. And with every move they made they realised that the passage hadn't been used for eons` as countless chunks of plaster that had dropped from the ceiling after years of neglect, lay scattered about the floor, along with the bones of long dead creatures, and droppings made by rodents that were living in the filthy, grime filled area. There were dust filled cobwebs that were combined into an interwoven mesh filling the vast area ahead of them that they couldn't see through.

"Oh blood hell!" Joan screeched when a fat arachnid began sliding down her face. "I can`t cope with this, there`s too much filth to get through, we shall have to go back and get something to get rid of these cobwebs. "You wait here."

"You are not leaving me with those things," Anne screeched, as her mother reopened the door.

Joan's patience was running thin with her daughters none-stop wittering. "Shut up, stop moaning and wait there," she snapped, holding the door to the canteen partially open. "Have you got a couple of brushes and candles and matches we could use?" she called to one of the nurses, who was staring at her in surprise by her unexpected dusty appearance. There are cobwebs and dirt everywhere," she explained brushing the repugnant creatures onto the floor from her hair and clothes.

"Yes," Nurse Baxter, was the first to overcome her surprise at seeing Joan, emerging so quickly from the corridor, and hurried over to the storage cupboard to find her the brushes and candles.

Joan nodded in gratification as another nurse handed her a box of matches. "Thank you, I will return everything when we have finished," Joan, attempted a smile that was more like a grimace, as she took the tackle from the nurses, and hurriedly closed the door then locked it, and almost fell over Anne, who was standing directly behind her.

"I wasn't waiting in there," she added harshly. "It's worse than I expected, anyway why do we need candles when we have torches?" she commented dryly, shining her lamp into the dismal darkness ahead.

"Because when I light the candle, the flame will burn through the cobwebs and destroy the insects living in the webs," Joan, explained.

"But won't it set the place on fire?"

"No, you, silly sod, the flame is not strong enough to do that, it will only sear through the cobwebs in front of us and give us a clear path along the corridor. Now come on let's get moving, the sooner we get started, then the sooner we will be out of here."

Joan, and Anne, gritted their teeth when the appalling stench of damp and decay filled their nostrils. Then holding the lighted candle in front of her with one hand, and using swinging motions with the brush in her other, Joan began leading the way forward through the dark, cold, vermin riddled corridor. And was constantly brushing aside the insect infested cobwebs that were strung above and all around them, while at the same time burning away the sticky tissue that clung to their clothing, and constantly tripping over huge lumps of plaster that had disgorged themselves from the ceiling and walls. There was no daylight from any window, as every one of them along the corridor was boarded up both inside and out, eradicating any form of light from entering the formidable area.

"My goodness do you recognise where we are?" Joan, suddenly stopped and shone her head-light onto the wooden structure alongside them.

"No, where are we?" Anne questioned. "We are near the dividing wall that is sealing the recreation area from the rear corridor."

"Oh, You`re right." Anne, replied eyeing the filth infested woodwork. "We`re halfway along the back of the hospital."

"Come on, let`s get moving," Joan, said as she turned her attention away from the wooden barrier, and resumed moving once more through the filthy cobwebs encrusted with dust and grime, that were hanging from the ceiling and spanning the entire width of the walls.

Anne, however, could hardly conceal her excitement, when the light from her torch picked up a door on the right hand side of the corridor.

"Mum! Look! There`s a door," she whispered, grabbing hold of Joan`s arm. "You`re right," Joan, replied, moving warily forward, swinging the brush in every direction, sending the insects scuttling into their nests. She could just make out in the murky darkness, a door set in the external wall at the far end of the corridor that must have led to the outside of the building. There was also another door built into the inner wall, where, as they drew closer, they could see a rickety wooden staircase leading upwards towards the first floor landing.

"This must have been the servants' entrance," Joan, assumed, brushing away and burning the grime covered cobwebs to enable her to see where she were going, while Anne, shone her torch light around the corridor.

"Mum, take a look at this " Anne, called excitedly.

"What have you found?"

"Look at these panels.

"For a few moments, Joan, stopped swinging the brush from side to side and came to her daughters side and held the candle closer to see what Anne had become so enthusiastic about.

"Feast your eyes on those," Anne, spoke excitedly, as she held the candle closer to singe more of the cobwebs away, then shone the light from her torch to reveal exotically carved wooden panels, reaching half way up the walls. "We didn't notice them earlier did we? We were too busy fighting off the spiders," she added smugly.

Joan, bent lower to examine the intricate carvings, then stood up shaking her head. "Some silly bugger has made a right mess of these," she remarked, and was infuriated when she saw seeing that the once beautifully carved decorations, were now practically unrecognizable.

The elaborate details of each figure and animal had been continuously covered by many layers of grossly coloured grey paint, and were now enveloped in a multi layered combination of mildew, cobwebs and filth, so that Joan, could barely make out what the figures were.

Then, when she shone her lamp up towards the ceiling, she gasped when she saw that the strip lighting that hadn't been used for years and must have been there from the nineteen seventies. The tubes of florescent lights were hanging precariously at various angles from the ceiling on long rusted chains.

Joan, was furious, "Why on earth didn't they do something to protect all of these valuable decorations? The wood panels alone must be worth a fortune. Surely they are not going to be left and bulldozed along with the house."

"The same thing crossed my mind when I noticed the parquet floors on the wards," Anne, commented, with a solemn expression on her face. "Have you noticed the wall paper."

Swinging the brush in all directions, Joan, made her way across the corridor to inspect the hand printed wallpaper, that had also been covered by numerous coats of emulsion paint over the years. This was now buried beneath a mass of cobwebs and was hanging in long inflexible strips away from the walls.

Also adding to the depressing atmosphere, they could just make out in the inky darkness, the ornate, antiquated, heavy duty radiators set at various intervals along the corridor. The pipes, Joan, decided would at one time would have heated the entire hospital, but they had now been dismantled and the remaining sections of piping and joints, were pitted with rust and flaking paint.

Joan, however, had been so busy concentrating on what she was looking at, jumped when Anne, unexpectedly grabbed hold of her arm. "Mum," she whispered, "I don`t want to alarm you but I think someone is following us."

"What! Are you sure?"

"Yes, I sensed it when we were examining the wall panels."

"Right."

Joan swung round lighting up the filthy corridor with the strong beam from her flashlight, and was surprised to see an elderly man standing in the darkness, shielding his eyes from the brilliant glare of her lamp.

"Take that bloody light away from my eyes" he grumbled, trying to move away from the glaring beam.

"Who are you? What are you doing here?" she demanded to know.

I`m Harry Johnson, the caretaker, and I should be asking the questions here, not you?" he demanded.

CHAPTER ELEVEN

WARNING FROM HARRY

"I'm Joan Shepherd, and this is my daughter Anne," she explained. "I was asked by the Board of Trustees to come and investigate the phenomena that is occurring here.

Harry`s, tone relaxed a little.`

Oh, right then," he mumbled. "Well I didn`t know who you were and I didn't want to frighten you, so I followed to see what you were up to. I can tell you now that you can`t get through them doors at the end of the passage without the keys from Matron."

"Keys? What keys? the Matron never said anything about locked doors, she said that we could move about freely, as long as we kept the door locked leading from the food hall."

"I wouldn`t take much notice on what that silly old cow say`s, she`s crackers, it comes from working with that lot for so long. Anyway you`re nearly at the door when you do get the keys, then ask her for the one that opens the barred gate at the bottom of the steps that leads down to the padded cells and operating theatres."

"Operating theatres?" Anne, asked in surprise, "You don't mean?"

"Yes I do, in the olden days the looneys were put in straightjackets and shackled to the walls in padded cells before they were operated on. That's how they managed to keep em quiet, drugged and operated on, I can tell you they were bloody cruel in them days."

"Good grief!" Anne, exclaimed. "Do they still operate on people here?" she asked, hardly daring to hear what Harry's answer would be.

"Not any more love," Harry's smile was genuine as he spoke. "Thank the lord they don't do that here anymore, but you don't know what the buggers are up to in other places, we do know this though." He tapped the side of his nose knowingly with his finger. "Worldwide the buggers are using us all in mass experiments, and they'll keep having wars and outbreaks of disease to keep the population down. Well," he snorted, "I've said me piece. I suppose I'd better be getting back on me rounds or Matron will be after my hide," he muttered dejectedly.

"Yes and we shall have to go back and get the keys from Matron." Anne, was peeved by the mere thought of having to fight their way back through the filthy corridor, and especially asking for anything from the odious woman.

"No" Joan, replied in a razor edged voice, she was annoyed at being unable to proceed any further along the building. "We may as well go upstairs and take a look at the empty wards," she grumbled, irritated by the inconvenience caused by the Matron's infuriating, obstructive, behaviour and pointed towards the old staircase. "Maybe we will find something up there."

"Just you be careful," Harry, motioned towards the dark wooden staircase with his lamp. "Them, stairs aren't safe," he warned. "And another thing, do you want to know why they put shutters and bars up at them windows, and closed off the top half of the building? I can tell you," He added, again giving a sly grin and patting the side of his nose with his grubby finger. "It was because too many of them silly buggers were either smashing the glass or cutting thersens. Or they were jumping off the balcony, that's why up there's closed off and not used.

CHAPTER TWELVE

THE STAIRCASE

Although deeply shocked by what Harry, had said, Anne, asked if there was anything else they needed to know.

"Oh for goodness sake Anne." Joan, stopped her from asking anymore questions. "I think we should go upstairs and take a look around, perhaps we may be able to see what we are doing up there, as there are plenty of windows and it is still daylight."

Anne, scowled at her mother, but didn't say another word and followed her when she walked towards the old staircase that was completely immersed beneath layers of cobwebs and filth.

However, the minute Joan, placed her hand on the paint peeling handrail, she felt it move, she then tried putting her weight onto the first two steps of the staircase, but quickly withdrew when feeling it sway and creak. "I don`t think these steps are safe to use," she muttered looking up and shining her lamp into the filthy encrusted darkness, where she could just make out through the thick layer of cobwebs and dust, that there were six broad steps leading to a small landing, then more steps, but she couldn't see where they led as it was too dark and her vision was blocked by the mass of cobwebs entwining the complete staircase.

"Damn," she snapped, irritated by the lack of light and the filth surrounding her. "This staircase is much narrower than the one in the entrance hall and it looks as if it`s got woodworm. So if we do decide to go up there, then we will have to be careful where we put our feet," Joan, remarked in an apprehensive tone.

"Be it on your own heads," Harry, mumbled, switching off his lamp, he then turned and walked away into the darkness.

For a few moments they stood uncertain of what to do next, until Anne, started complaining again that she was cold. "Blood hell mother, can`t we go back its f------- freezing down here."

"Don't you dare use that word in my presence," Joan, snapped at her daughter, "I have enough of that from your father." She then turned to shine the flashlight along the entire length of the squalid, dark, corridor and squinted in the darkness unable to see very far, as the grime encrusted cobwebs suspended from the ceiling, criss-crossing from either side of the corridor was blocking her vision

Anne, however, could feel the goosebumps rising all over her body, and couldn`t say for certain if it was from the cold, or the fear of what could be in the corridor upstairs waiting for them. "Why do we have to go this way, it`s not safe?" she grumbled. "Why can`t we go back and use the main staircase to get to the first floor?"

"We can`t get that way because of the barrier, you, silly girl," her mother retorted irritably, annoyed by her daughter`s constant complaining.

"Well I don`t see why they couldn't at least have had the electricity switched on for us to see where we were going," Anne, commented loudly, triggering her voice to echo eerily along the dark corridor. Then slid to a halt and almost choked on her words when seeing the ghostly apparition of a monk surrounded by a halo of pale grey light, gliding silently along the corridor towards them. But before it drew close, it turned at a slight angle and disappeared through the wall directly in front of it.

"Mum," she whispered, frantically pulling at her mother`s arm. "Mum, I just saw something go through that wall down there"

41

"So did I," Joan answered softly, "but don`t worry about it right now, we can check it out later."

"But mum."

"Anne," she spoke in an appeasing tone, "whoever it was will be long gone by now, so put it out of your mind and concentrate on what you are doing now."

"But mum."

"Oh for goodness` sake."

Ignoring her mother`s comments, Anne, cautiously moved over to where the apparition had disappeared and began examining the wall, then without turning she called to her mother to come and take a look at the wall where the phantom had vanished. "It must have entered the back of the recreation room," Anne, whispered excitedly.

"You`re right," Joan, replied, "come on we will check the out the recreation room later, after we`ve been upstairs."

"You mean we are going to risk climbing that dangerous staircase?" Anne, stared at her mother in disbelief.

"Of course I am, are you coming with me or are you waiting here."

"Only if you go first," Anne, replied, determined not to be left behind, "anyway you don`t know what could be waiting for us up there."

Joan, gave a grim smile and moved towards the staircase, but the moment she placed her hand onto the wobbly hand rail, to her horror, an assortment of creepy crawlies raced over her gloves and quickly burrowed beneath them and crept over her skin. "Oh my goodness," she shrieked, pulling the gloves away from her hands when feeling the parasites bite into her skin, she began screaming and leaping about like a demented idiot and threw her gloves onto the floor and stamped on them, hoping to crush whatever was inside.

"Mum, leave it, you can`t wear them again," Anne, declared loudly trying to make herself heard above the racket her mother was making.

"What?"

"I said you can`t wear those gloves, so calm down and get hold of yourself, "

Filled with revulsion by the sickening experience, Joan shone her lamp onto the handrail and was nauseated when seeing that the splintered woodwork was infested with bugs crawling over everything in sight.

"Mum what are we going to do?" Anne asked in dismay.

Joan, thought for a moment, then relit the candle and indicated for Anne, to do likewise. She next switched off her torch and fastened it to the fitment on her belt, then together they held the flames from both candles beneath the cobwebs and scorched the bugs away from the hand rail.

Once that was cleared, Joan held the candle before her and started climbing the creaking staircase, and with her other hand she used the long handled brush to sweep aside the aphids nesting in the dusty cobwebs that were encompassing the whole area from top to bottom, but with both hands engaged in clearing the way, in the dark, it wasn't easy. While at the same time, she had to watch where she was putting her feet, as the rubble that had fallen from the ceiling lay scattered across the steps. Consequently it was virtually impossible for Joan, to see where she was treading, she was also using her headlamp to allow her to use her hands in case of the staircase collapsing.

CHAPTER THIRTEEN

THE TREACHEROUS STAIRCASE.

With only the beam from her headlamp to direct her, Joan, took a cautious step forward, then stopped when noticing how badly warped and cracked the bare timbers were. Large running splits laid bare, three inch wide gaps in the wood, and missing steps revealing gaping black holes stayed her from going any further.

Anne, was also aware of the dangerous situation and called to her mother that it would be too dangerous for her to proceed. But Joan, who was stubborn, refused to give in to anything or anyone, ignored her warning and cautiously moved forward, and spread eagled her legs, so that she was placing her weight equally onto either side of the first two steps, that groaned and creaked immediately she put her weight on them.

"Oh for goodness` sake." Anne, griped, and with her heart in her mouth, she watched as her mother tested the strength of each step, before moving forward onto the next then screamed when she heard a loud crack. "Oh my God!" She shrieked when in the torch light she saw her mother drop the brush when the rotten timber gave way beneath her feet and grab hold of the handrail to steady herself. "Mother, come back," she yelled.

But Joan, was determined to climb the stairs, clinging precariously to the unsteady hand rail, and disregarding the stinging pain in her leg, she hoisted herself up over the damaged step until finally reaching the swaying landing.

"Anne, it`s alright," she called shining her lamp down onto her daughter`s worried face.

"The staircase is breaking away from the wall, the cement has rotted away from between the stone, so be very careful when you come up, and bring the brush with you."

`*Bloody marvellous*,` Anne, muttered to herself. *"Bring the f------- brush never mind me*," she grumbled. "I`m going to throw the brush up mum, you catch it, I can`t get up there safely holding the bloody brush can I?"

"Well, switch your bloody headlamp back on, then you can see what you`re doing," Joan, shouted, "ready when you are!"

Seething, Anne, took hold of the brush and hurled it up towards her mother, who caught it first try, then after switching on her head lamp and holding the glowing candle in front of her, she clipped the main torch to her belt and with a thudding heart she moved towards the first step. "Right, I`m coming up mum, but if at any moment I feel that it`s not safe enough, then I won`t be taking any chances and I will be staying put, do you understand?"

"Don`t worry sweetheart," Joan, called from the darkness above. "I do understand, now come on and keep to the side nearest the wall, just remember you`re heavier than me and let your headlight show you where to tread. The third and fifth steps are missing so count them as you come up."

"Does she always have to keep reminding me of my weight?" Anne, fumed, then froze when the minute she stepped onto the staircase she felt it move. `Oh crumbs,` she murmured softly, then trying hard to conquer her fear, Anne, gradually made her way up the rickety, unstable staircase until reaching her mother on the platform, between the two sets of stairs.

In the meantime, Joan, had brushed and singed away as many cobwebs and insects that she could reach, but when she had shone the light onto the remaining stairs, Joan, felt a sickening sensation in the pit in her stomach, when noticing that three of the steps were missing.

"Anne, I am going to give you the opportunity to make up your own mind, you can either go back down the staircase or____"

"Don`t say any more mother, whatever you do I do."

"Are you certain?"

"I`m not leaving you on your own, if anything happened to you, then dad would never forgive me. That`s if he hadn't killed me first."

"Come on then, I`ll go first and when I reach the top, you get up there as fast as you can. I don`t like the feel of this part of the staircase, it`s too unstable for my liking."

"Huh now she thinks it`s not safe, when we`ve got this far," Anne mumbled to herself.

"Once we`re up we will go back down on the main staircase, I`m not risking this one, again, her mum said, giving her a smile of encouragement.

"Huh, that`s if we manage to get up these steps first," Anne grumbled .

CHAPTER FOURTEEN

THE GHOSTLY SUICIDE

After a few hair raising incidents, they managed to reach the balcony in comparative safety, where they became aware that the insignificant beam of light permeating from the grimy window at the top of the stairs, didn`t give them much scope to see where they were heading, compelling them to switch on their main flashlights.

To their dismay however, they were appalled when stepping onto the balcony, to find themselves standing almost ankle deep in multi layers of debris and filth. Even more frustrating, was that after struggling to reach the nearest door and endeavouring to open it, they found that it was swollen and stuck tight. It was obviously due to the years of neglect that the damp caused, by the lack of heating! and the rubble piled up at the back of the doors was causing a major problem.

Joan, however, was used to handling tricky situations like this, and using all the force she could Joan, pushed and shoved until she managed to get the door open wide enough for them to squeeze through.

But within minutes of entering the room, a mass of screeching rats and mice which had lived undisturbed in the squalid region for many years, scattered in all directions in a desperate attempt to get out of range of their lights. The rodents had scrambled over their feet to race past them, panicking at the sight of humans who posed a great threat to them.

Nevertheless, Joan, and Anne, screamed and hopped from one leg to another, when the odious vermin leapt over their feet and didn't stop until the room was clear of them. "Shit, I didn't expect this" Anne, shrieked, clinging hold of her mother.

"Neither did I!" Joan, squealed, trembling all over.

"I'll stay here, while you take a look round," Anne, said, pushing her mother into the repugnant space.

"Thanks," Joan, muttered, turning to face her daughter, "thanks a million. "Nevertheless, despite the shock of coming into such close contact with the pest riddled infestation, Joan, guardedly, edged her way into the rank, stinking room, taking care to avoid standing in the vermin's excrement, the skeleton remains of their prey and the lumps of fallen plaster, as she headed towards the window. There she observed, that the steel wire mesh protecting the glass from breakage, was entwined with cobwebs and dust, as were the steel bars, that were bolted in front and the outside of the huge French window leading onto the balcony.

Within minutes, Joan, recalled what Harry, the caretaker had told them, the steel wire mesh had been set in front of the windows to stop the patients from smashing the glass and injuring themselves, and the bars were there to stop them from walking out onto the balcony and leaping to their deaths.

`My goodness! How awful! Those poor unfortunate souls must have been desperate to do a thing like that*, she pondered, then gasped and took a step back from the window, when observing something bizarre was about to take place. "Anne, quick, come over here," Joan, called to her daughter, indicating for her to see what she was looking at. "You've got to see this."

"What is it?" Anne, whispered, scrambling over to her mum's side. "Oh my God!" she exclaimed loudly, when seeing the figure of a woman climbing over the balcony railings. "What do you think she's doing?" "It's obvious," Joan, said softly. "She is about to jump."

"Can't we stop her," "Don't be silly, she's a ghost." No sooner than she'd spoken, the woman disappeared over the iron balcony.

"Mum!" Anne, cried in alarm.

"It's too late, she's gone," Joan, said taking hold of Anne's hand. "I told you it was a ghost, didn't I?"

"Yes, but."

"Never mind the but's, come on, there's nothing we can do to help her, so let's get on and check the other rooms, that's if we can get into them, then we can go up to the next floor."

"For goodness' sake mum," Anne, snapped, "stop acting like a heartless bitch, think of that poor woman."

Joan, turned to her daughter with an irritated look on her face. "Listen to me Anne, in this line of work you must realise that you can't change what has happened in the past, we are here to help the living, who are experiencing problems with the deceased, who do not realise they are dead, do you understand?"

"Yes," Anne, mumbled, shuffling her feet amongst the debris, accepting that Joan, was corret in what she was saying.

"Right then!" Let's get on with the job we were paid to do, and that is to help the living."

CHAPTER FIFTEEN

A BRIEF RESPITE

By pushing forcefully at the doors, they eventually managed to enter each room, but found that every one of them was entirely infested with the filth, vermin and debris that had amassed over the years. The rooms were also devoid of any furnishings, and were in an identical crumbling and stinking condition as the rest. Also there was no sign of any psychic activity.

"Well, seeing that nothing is happening here, I think we should take a short rest before going any further," Joan, declared wearily, while at the same time checking her watch. " My goodness," she gasped, when seeing that it was two thirty in the afternoon, "I had completely forgotten about lunch. I think we should have something to eat," she remarked, opening the pack of sandwiches. "You pour the flask of coffee we brought with us, then afterwards, if you feel up to it we can check out the second floor. Or would you rather we return to our room?" Joan, asked.

"No, let`s have our sandwiches then carry on, " Anne, replied. "There is just one problem mum though," she remarked, shining her lamp about the squalid messy floor. "There`s nowhere we can sit down to eat, everything is filthy."

"Don`t worry about it," Joan replied, picking up the large sweeping brush. "I`ll sweep the top step of the main staircase, it will be a bit dusty, but we will be able to sit down and have a break for a short while. We both need a rest, I don`t know about you? But I`m as hungry as a horse."

"You`re always hungry mum," Anne, remarked, with a disparaging snigger, and waited as her mother swept away the debris from the centre of the wide staircase. To be honest after the climb up that precariously swinging staircase and striving to get a foothold between the missing steps. They had both found the effort physically and mentally exhausting, nevertheless Anne, readily agreed to them checking out the second floor after they had rested for a while.

However, while they were sitting eating the sandwiches, and drinking hot coffee from the flask cups, Anne, who had been shining her light about the surrounding area, noticed that only a few feet away from where they were sitting, was another staircase at the far end of the balcony and nudged her mother.

"Look," she said, shining the light towards the staircase, "there`s another set of stairs and they aren't connected to the ones we`ve just climbed. Do you think it could possibly be another part of the servants` staircase? After all, they are at the rear of the house and from here it looks pretty solid.

"You could be right," Joan replied getting to her feet. "Come on let`s take a look. But I promise you this, if it is unstable and unsafe in any way, then we are not going anywhere near it."

The old floorboards creaked, and clouds of dust rose as they moved steadily forward, crunching the skeletal remains of long dead creatures and vermin droppings beneath their feet as they made their way over to the abandoned staircase. "It looks safe enough," she said when reaching it and shone her lamp up towards the next landing. "None of the steps are missing," she added thoughtfully, "shall I give it a try?" Anne, nodded her head in agreement. Joan, took that as a yes, and got hold of the banister rail that appeared to be much firmer and sturdier than the one they had previously held and checked it for movement! thankfully the timber was securely affixed into the wall. She next tested the steps, but because of the dryness in them, she hesitated when they began to creak and groan when putting her weight on them. To her relief though, they didn't crack or splinter beneath her feet nor were any of the steps broken or missing.

Feeling confident, Joan, swept and burnt away the masses of cobwebs and bulbus insects before making her way up the first eight set of steps, until reaching the central platform. She then called down to Anne, that it was safe for her to come up, but with every step Anne, took, she couldn't bring herself to relax, until reaching the ledge where her mother was waiting. They next made their way up the rest of the stairs, until reaching the balcony above on the second floor level.

By now however, although it was only four thirty, the darkness had closed in and they found themselves standing in an area that was pitch black. The slight amount of light that had come from the high circular window had disappeared beneath the heavy clouds that were forming, indicated that another storm was approaching. Nevertheless they once again found themselves walking through fallen debris, vermin droppings and small skeletal remains, that cracked as the bones shattered beneath their feet.

Using both strong beams of light to illuminate the whole area ahead, Joan, and Anne, could see that there was a significant number of intimidating, spooky, dark corridors wending their way between the rooms alongside the stretch of balcony. "Do you think we should go down one of those corridors?" Anne, asked, guardedly hoping that her mother would say no and stay on the balcony.

To her profound relief ,Joan, preferred to investigate the rooms where she could see there was a number of open doors. However, as they approached the first open room Joan, felt a sneaking suspicion that something didn't feel right and turned to Anne. "Something`s wrong here," she whispered, "do you want to continue? if not then we can go back?"

"It`s alright mum," Anne, replied, keeping her voice low, "I understand what you`re saying, I can feel it as well."

Joan, nodded. "Follow me then, but stay close."

CHAPTER SIXTEEN

REALIZATION

"What do you think mum?" Anne tried to keep the quiver out of her voice as she spoke."

"I don`t think anything, but I know what I am going to do." Joan, replied as she pushed the partially open door wide enough for them both to pass through. "Oh my God," she uttered silently, where seeing in the thick layers of grime on the floor, were a number of bird and animal skeletons scattered in disarray amongst the debris. "It looks as if someone has been living here," she mumbled, then felt her heart thud and leap in alarm, when masses of squeeling rodents leapt and jumped over her feet, in an effort to escape the unwelcome intruder.

"Bloody hell mother! I can`t stand much more of this!" Anne, screamed, using her torch to swipe away the obnoxious creatures that were clinging to her jeans.

"It`s alright, love," Joan, whispered reassuringly, as she placed a comforting hand on Anne`s trembling arm. "Let`s get back to the balcony, there`s something I want to take a good look at."

Anne`s fears were quickly dispelled by her mother`s reassuring words, and allowed herself to be guided back along the corridor to the balcony, where the powerful beam from her mother`s torch lit up six open doors, three in front of them and three behind.

"Anne."

"What?"

"When we went along that corridor, we didn't reach the end did we?"

"No."

"That's what I thought."

"Why do you ask?"

"Well, we counted three doors on either side of the corridor on the balcony, yet when we went along the corridor we could see that there were more rooms and corridors further along wasn't there?"

"You're right mum, the nurses' quarters are on the ground floor, the canteen, and the patients' recreation room, then there is the passage where we came up the servants' staircase. On the other side, is the reception area, four Women's wards, and behind those are the four Men's wards, a treatment room and the rear passage."

"Blinking heck, that means that there are more rooms here than what we anticipated."

"Come on," Joan's voice was urgent as she spoke. "I think we should inspect the rooms on the Balcony, then return to our quarter's and get cleaned up for supper."

CHAPTER SEVENTEEN

PHENOMENA

To their surprise however, every room they passed leading from the balcony was ankle deep in muck and filth. Then to make matters worse all of the rooms they checked, had heavy layers of dust and cobwebs covering obsolete hospital and medical equipment that was entirely masked by the grime covering them. Empty storage cabinets, wheelchairs, bed frames, damaged lockers, metal trays still containing syringes, scalpels, even thread for stitching up lacerations, and stands for supporting drips, fridges, etc filled every room they investigated.

"It looks as if all of the rooms up here were used for storage only," Anne, assumed, when observing the discarded medical equipment scattered about the cluttered spaces.

"You could be right," Joan, agreed.

However, in the last remaining debris littered room they entered, they spotted an ancient relic from the past. It was an antique, wicker wheelchair with a long, metal, steering handle at the front, that was parked at the far corner of the room. Nearby was a broken spring` based bedstead and a locker minus it`s door, apart from those articles, the room was devoid of anything else.

"I`ve never seen one of those before" Anne exclaimed with a huge smile on her face and went over with Joan, to take a good look at it. But while their attention was taken by the ancient relic, unnoticed by both women, a dark shadow had flitted across the bare floorboards behind them and was now stood watching them from the doorway.

"I can`t hazard a guess at how much these fireplaces must be worth?" Joan, said, walking over to the ornately carved, pure white, marble structures, and brushing the dust and cobwebs away, she revealed the perfectly carved contours of two scantily clad women bearing the full weight of the of ledge above.

"Quite a bit," Anne, replied, "and I wish I had a figure like that," she mumbled, looking down at her own bulky form. "Mum, did you notice the door that we came through?"

"I can`t say I did," Joan, replied, "I was too busy concentrating on what was in the room and it was too dark for me to notice anything else."

"Well there were carved panels on the interior, but I couldn't make out what the carvings were?" "No, but I did notice the ones on the outside of the door, but I was too busy trying to see where I was putting my feet when we entered the room, we can examine them later," she added.

Anne gazed about the spacious room and observed that the ornate plaster that had broken away from the ceiling, was now lying shattered on the floor along with chunks of intricately carved cornice. While below, the expensive Victorian wallpaper that had been repeatedly painted over by layers of cheap emulsion paint, was now hanging in long wide strips away from the walls and was propping up years of grime and dirt.

All of a sudden the unexpected occurred, when without warning an unpleasant putrid stench of decomposition began filling their nostrils, along with the lingering stench of chlorine based chemicals, medical and human body waste that had suddenly arisen and was almost chocking them.

Gagging and spluttering, Joan, yelled for Anne, to cover her nose and mouth with something, anything and get out of there."

However, as Joan, attempted to escape, she felt herself being pushed to the floor by an invisible assailant and the torch was pulled from her grasp, she then heard it clatter onto the floor and to her horror it switched itself off, leaving her blind and helpless in the eerie surroundings.

Meanwhile, as she struggled to breath, upon hearing the commotion, Anne, had turned to shine her torch over to where her mother had fallen and saw that she was struggling to get to her feet. Whereby Anne, realising the predicament her mother was in, hurried to Joan`s, side and helped her up, yet when they searched for her torch it had gone, there was no sign of it. While at the same time they were totally unaware of the spectral figure that had followed them from the first floor, was now standing beside them.

"Mum," Anne whispered uncertainly.

"What?"

"There`s a man in here watching us."

No sooner had she spoken, when all hell broke loose, the broken locker that had been leant against the wall opposite from where they were standing, unexpectedly spun towards them, forcing Joan, to push Anne, to one side, then leap out of the way as it shot past, narrowly missing her by inches.

"Oh my God, that was close," she yelled turning towards her daughter, then let out a scream of warning, when lumps of plaster came crashing down from the ceiling narrowly missing their heads. But before they had the time to recover, they found themselves enveloped in a massive cloud of soot and dust that had cascaded down from the chimney. The revolting stinking matter instantly spread across the whole of the room, filling the entire floor space with a suffocating stench, then as the gaseous substance spread across the floor it began drifting up towards the ceiling.

"Oh my God mum look!" Anne, shrieked, aiming her torch towards a number of shadowy figures that had formed in the dense substance, and watched horrified as they floated up towards the ceiling and vanished into the dark surroundings.

"Enough is enough," Joan, spluttered, dragging her shaking daughter by the arm. "We are getting out of here."

Coughing and choking, they staggered backwards towards the door, then cried out in alarm when it slammed shut and the key turned in the lock.

"Mam we`re trapped, what are we going to do?" Anne, screamed. "Don`t panic, I told you before, if it`s a bad entity, then it will feed on your fear. So try to remain calm and control yourself if you can."

Joan, began pulling at the door handle and kicked at the door itself, but the solid mahogany door was impregnable and refused to move. "Shit, what do we do now?" she muttered to herself, then felt a tremor of alarm run through her, when recalling that there had been no key in the lock on either side of the door, when they had entered the room the door had been wide open.

CHAPTER EIGHTEEN

TRAPPED

"We have got to get out of here, can you see another door? "Anne didn't hear her mother calling to her, she was almost beside herself with fear as the daunting notion of being trapped with unseen forces was sweeping through her mind and paralyzing her movements.

"Anne!" she heard her mother yell. "Pull yourself together, this is no time for stupid dramatics, I haven't got a torch to see what I`m doing, so get your act together and find another way out!"

Joan`s, frenzied words promptly drew Anne, out of her catatonic state. "I can`t," she whimpered, scanning the room for another door.

Within seconds of them realising there was no escape, the temperature began to plunge at a terrifying rate. But when seeing the freezing cold breath exuding from their mouths and nostrils, which was turning into frosty puffs of air, Anne, began to panic.

"Heaven help us," Joan, whispered softly, when sensing something bad was about to happen. In an effort to protect her daughter, Joan, grabbed hold of her and held her close and grabbed the torch from her quivering hands and began silently praying. Surprisingly at that moment the dust began evaporating and in a dazzling beam of light, they observed a short, thin man slowly emerge dressed in a hospital gown.

"Oh my God," Joan, whispered, staring in awe at the chilling sight, then without thinking she began to pray out loud.

As if by magic her prayers were answered, when to her relief the apparition suddenly disappeared, the air became clear and the temperature returned to normal, then adding to her bewilderment, the locked door unexpectedly swung silently open.

"Mum," Anne, whispered nervously, maintaining the grip on her mother`s arm. I think we should leave now while we can, don`t you?" she declared."

"Yes," Joan, replied, "I think we`ve had enough for one day. Let`s get out while we can, I think they should get the clergy in to sort this mess out, to be honest it`s beyond me," Joan, declared as she ushered her daughter away from the bizarre room and down the main staircase.

"The whole building needs an exorcism."

CHAPTER NINETEEN.

SAFE RETURN

Subsequently, since the traumatic events that had occurred while investigating the second floor, and being trapped in a room where the bizarre phenomena had taken place. Joan, and Anne, hadn't realised how quickly the time had passed, and by the time they reach the safety of the staff canteen, it was almost seven pm in the evening.

Consequently, immediately they entered the canteen, doctor and nurses alike stopped talking and stared at their dishevelled appearances. "Are you alright?" Sister Darwin asked hurrying to Joan and Anne's side when seeing their ashen faces and dust covered clothing.

"Yes," Joan replied, "we need to go to our room and get cleaned up. Afterwards we will tell you what happened up there." Ignoring the nurse's curious stares and offers of help, they hurried to their room to remove their dirty clothes. All modesty was forgotten, as they stripped off their underwear. Anne, leapt into the shower and turned on the flow of hot heat and watched as the grime and filth from her hair and body swirled away down the plug hole. Joan meanwhile had submerged herself into a tub full of scalding hot water to remove the bugs from her irritated skin and head. It must have taken almost an hour before they felt clean again and towelled themselves dry with the warm towels from the heated rails.

"Let's go get something warm to eat, then we can come back and have an early night," Joan proposed to Anne, who was exhausted. She just nodded in agreement as she dressed herself in clean clothing.

"Do you think there are any fleas on our clothes?" she asked, pointing to the discarded garments lying on the floor.

"It`s highly probable," Joan, replied, opening the door and kicking the heap of bug riddled gear away from the room into the hallway. "We can sort them out tomorrow, but right now I`m famished."

"So am I," Anne, replied. "After we`ve eaten, I think we should go to bed."

CHAPTER TWENTY

THE HAUNTED PATH AND HOUSE

"Would you like to take a walk?" Joan, asked, as they were sitting having breakfast the following morning. "Maybe getting outdoors for a while, the fresh air will clear our heads instead of being couped up inside the hospital?" she suggested.

"I'm glad you proposed that Mum! By the way did you notice that someone had removed our dirty clothes from outside our room last night," Anne said casually, as she scraped the jam pot clean with her knife and lathered it over the last slice of toast.

Joan groaned inwardly, why did Anne have to be so like her father and keep eating until there was nothing left on the table? She had already eaten a huge English breakfast, now she was pushing extra slices of toast down her throat. "Yes I did, and there was a note pushed under the door to say that our clothing had been taken for cleaning. Perhaps we could take a walk down the path leading to the main road," Joan hinted, changing the subject and looking away from her daughter, so that she didn't have to watch her eat so much. "You know, the one where the nurses have felt someone following and touching them."

"Huh, I knew there would be a catch somewhere," Anne, replied, wiping her mouth on the napkin and getting to her feet. "Come on then, what are we waiting for?" she leant across the table to take the uneaten half slice of buttered toast from her mum's plate. "Let's get going."

Dressed in warm clothing and armed with cameras strapped around their necks, they set off into the fast falling snow. As luck would have it, most of the snow had been cleared from the drive, but was piled high on both sides of the footpath. Nevertheless, although it had been gritted, it was still slippery underfoot and with the force of the howling wind, they soon found themselves hanging onto one another, as they struggled to stay upright against each billowing gusts.

Clinging to one another for support, they kept going along the slippery road until coming to the narrow footpath, which the staff used as a short cut to reach the main road. But to their dismay, when reaching the path, they found that it hadn`t been cleared and was more than ankle deep with snow and covered with patches of slippery ice and overgrown frozen weeds.

To make matters worse, the unkempt hedges sprouting shoulder high, thorny hawthorn branches constantly snagged at their clothing as they made their way along the glassy downhill gradient. The trees, now stripped bare of foliage with overhanging broughs, converged overhead in a tangled web, creating an obscure darkness on the already shaded path. Alongside this was a dense mass of protruding, unkempt evergreen bushes that grew wild on either side of the icy path, making it extremely difficult to pass through without becoming entangled in their prickly branches.

The combination of what they had heard about the phantom stalker, and the grim scary atmosphere on the murky, twisting path, did nothing to alleviate their concerns. Nor did it conceal the undisputed sense of vulnerability they were both feeling at that moment.

"Do you think we ought to go back?" Anne was visibly shaking as she spoke."

"Don`t be silly," Joan replied, even so, she was having second thoughts at the prospect of going any further away from the security of the hospital.

Before she could add anything further, Anne suddenly stopped to place a restraining hand on her mother's arm. "Mum, did you hear that?"

"Hear what? all I can hear is the wind," Joan, replied, pushing the wild brambles from her face.

"No it's not the wind! Listen! As we get further along the path the sound it's getting louder. I'm Scared, so I'm not going any further," Anne, whispered fearfully, peering from side to side. It was obvious that Anne, could hear something, when she refused to go any further along the path and was ready to turn and run.

Joan, however, did her best to calm her daughter, even so, Anne's, anxiety was starting to rub off onto her. "For goodness, sake Anne, there's nothing to be afraid of, what you're hearing is only the wind rustling through the tree branches, the rest is your imagination."

"No it isn't, just stand still and listen will you?" she snapped.

"All right then," Joan, replied in a pacifying tone and loosened the flap that was covering her ears so that she could hear, and stood listening for a few moments, before realising what was creating the noise.

On the plan of the old hospital, situated near the area where they were standing, it showed there was a generator that had powered the hospital with electricity and had been built in a location just a few yards away from the main building. The steady humming sound that Anne, was hearing, was emanating from that.

"It's alright, it is only the old generator," Joan, explained refastening her hat and moving over to the thick evergreen bushes, that she parted to expose the rusty antiquated generator, which was partially concealed amongst the evergreens and dead foliage.

"Oh good grief, I thought it was,-----"

"Well it isn't," Joan, stood shaking her head and almost laughed at the sight of her daughter as she stood quaking with fear.

"Well isn't this where the nurses said that someone was following them?" Anne asked, glancing behind to ensure no one was loitering behind them.

"That's what they have said," Joan replied. "Not only that, but one of the residents living nearby, actually saw a UFO land and take off in a field near his home. Ever since that incident the grass has never grown there again. And when the UFO landed it scared the hell out of his dog."

"Really?"

"Yes really."

"Mum?"

"What?"

"Is this somewhere close to where the haunted house is? You know the one that they used for making a film about terrorists? I heard that it's haunted and is constantly struck by lightning?"

"I believe so," Joan replied, "It is said to have lightning rods on every chimney." She then paused for a few moments and looked in the direction her daughter was pointing. But she couldn't see anything through the confines of the hedgerow because of its height surrounding them, plus there was also the twist and turns of the narrow lane to consider, that was blocking her line of vision.

"I have heard," Joan, commented, "that residents in the local area have seen lighted candles moving about on various floors of the derelict building at around midnight and have called the police. But when the police have investigated the house, they have found no trace of anyone having been in there. Now let's get moving and forget about ghosts and concentrate on what we came out here to do, that is to relax and take it easy for a while."

CHAPTER TWENTY ONE

THE WATERMILL

"Mum?"

"What?"

"Do you think it was the spirits of the mentally ill who were causing the phenomena yesterday?"

"Most likely," her mum replied, "I can`t see anyone in their right mind causing the danger that we were in, can you?"

"No."

Lost in thought, they walked in silence until coming to what should have been the main road, but now it was lost from sight, buried beneath a deep covering of snow.

"Where now?" Anne asked as they ground to a halt. "Haven`t they heard of snow ploughs out here in North Yorkshire?" she grumbled loudly.

"Never mind the road, let`s go over there, it looks interesting," Joan, remarked when noticing through the light peppering of falling snow, the faint outline of a derelict stone building in the far distance.

As usual, Anne, grumbled as she waded through the deep snow behind her mother, until reaching a ruined, disused water mill, where the deluge of rapidly flowing water surged directly ahead, and in an instant she became acutely alert. "I don`t think it is safe here mother? You can see where the banking has been washed away by the height of the surging river?"

"Nonsense," Joan, replied. "Let me tell you something."

"Oh no, not another one of you're know all `lectures," Anne, groaned.

"Just shut up and learn, instead of rambling all the time," Joan, snapped. "This is the River Wharfedale, and when the rivers get high, they open the floodgates on higher ground simultaneously to avoid flooding, before the water reaches Bolton Abbey that feeds the Strid. In days gone by," she continued knowingly.

"Oh no, here we go again," Anne, muttered rolling her eyes.

Joan, ignored her. "In days gone by, the Strid was where the toffs would try to show how clever and brave they were to the young ladies, by leaping across the rocks where there is a deep whirlpool. Some of them slipped and fell into the Strid`s notorious black hole and their bodies were never recovered. Even up to today, some silly buggers still try doing it and end up lost somewhere in the Strid`s bottomless whirlpool."

"I`m not certain if there is any truth in it or not," she carried on. "But I was told that it had been used for diving practice by certain government organisations. But when the divers started disappearing, they began carrying out their practice`s elsewhere."

"Mum that`s gross, but I have heard it all before, after all, I do live in Harrogate."

"Maybe so, but that`s what I`ve heard."

Anne, just shook her head and rolled her eyes, she didn't say another word. `What can you say` she thought to herself, `indeed what can you say to someone who thinks they know it all?`.

CHAPTER TWENTY TWO

HARRY

"I think we should be going back, the snow is getting heavier," Anne, commented when glancing around and observing that the whole countryside was slowly disappearing beneath a heavy blanket of freshly falling snow.

"You`re right," Joan, acknowledged, forcing her attention away from the old water mill. "I can`t see the hospital can you?"

Anne, fought to keep the sudden alarm she was feeling under control. No, and I can`t even remember what direction we came from."

"Bloody Hell," Joan, cursed at the absurd situation they found themselves in, when seeing that their footprints had been obliterated by the snow.

"Oh mum, what are we going to do now?"

"Stay calm and think, if we turn towards the direction we came from, then we can retrace our steps."

"Mum, we`ve both been walking around the old mill for ages and our footprints have already disappeared, if we set off walking then we could end up anywhere!"

"Damn! You`re right, but we can`t stand still, otherwise we will freeze to death out here."

"Yes and we didn't tell anyone where we were going, and if they do notice that we are missing, I don`t think that bitch of a Matron will send anyone searching for us."

"Oh Hell. What a bloody mess." Just then they heard a voice they recognised calling to them. "Listen! It's Harry, the caretaker, but what's he doing out here.

"Stay where you are ladies," he called, "keep shouting and I'll find you."

"Harry, thank goodness, we are lost!" Anne, yelled.

"Not for long," Harry, bellowed, as his bulky figure and a bright light slowly emerged through the falling snow. He was carrying an oil lamp affixed to the top of a shepherds, crook, and was barely recognisable beneath the bundle of thick clothing he was wearing. A deerstalker cap was tightly pulled around his head and underneath, he wore a thick balaclava to protect his face from the harsh winds and icy snow. If it hadn't been for his voice, they would never have recognised him.

"You shouldn't have wandered this far away from the hospital I saw you leave and followed, I knew you'd get lost," he chided. It's the worse snow storm we've had in years, now keep close and follow me," he grunted, holding the lamp high so that they could see it's dim outline ahead. It took almost three quarters of an hour stumbling every step of the way through the deep snow until they were safely back on the partially cleared road.

"Thanks Harry, you're an angel," Joan, said, giving him a hug of gratitude. "Don't talk daft," he mumbled, shrugging her arms away. "I've got to finish my rounds out here, then I can get back inside and have a tot to warm myself up." He gave them a sly grin. "Then a nice warm pot of tea and put my feet up for a couple of hours before I start inside. I will warn you though," he added in a cautious tone. "Be careful in ward four, that's then men's ward, and never go into the basement it's a hell hole down there. If you do decide to go down, just look through the gate but don't go inside, I did it once and I'll never do it again. Take my word for it, you will see things in there, that you'll wish you never had seen."

After giving them the warning, he trotted off and was soon hidden from sight by the howling storm and snow blizzard.

CHAPTER TWENTY THREE

THE APPERITION

Anne, bought two sandwiches and two slabs of cake from the staff canteen and had took them back to the room, while Joan, prepared the coffee she had brought with her in her own percolator, that was now bubbling away and filling the room with its delicious coffee aroma. She had mentioned before they set off for the Grange, that the coffee would be of a low grade, and she was right, the hospital coffee tasted like dish water.

As they ate, Anne, watched as Joan, constantly checked the time on the wall clock, that seemed to pass slower instead of faster, as they waited impatiently to begin the investigation that night. Then, when the clock coincided with her watch at ten fifteen pm, Joan, promptly turned to Anne.

"It`s time we started preparing ourselves! Strap the camera and the night lights to your head, then you`re hands are free to carry the infrared camcorder, and fix the flashlight to your accessory belt."

"Yes mother," Anne ,replied, watching as her mother did the same. Nevertheless she couldn`t help sensing the tension in her mother`s voice, but didn't ask what was troubling her.

"Are you ready?" Joan, asked, turning to face Anne.

"As ready as I`ll ever be," Anne, replied, giving her mother an assertive smile.

Joan, opened the door, "Right then, let`s get started."

Together they confidently made their way to the first ward, where they were met by Sister James, who was apparently nervous of what they were about to do. "Please be as quick and as quiet as you can. I don`t want the patients disturbing." she expressed in concern as she ushered them inside.

"Is this the only ward where the patients have seen the phantom figures?" Anne, asked softly, as she glanced around every corner of the dimly lit ward.

"No, the patients on all four wards have seen them," the Sister replied. "And one of the apparitions isn't always a pleasant sight," she hesitated for a moment. "A number of the night duty nurses have seen them, but." Sister James suddenly stopped herself from saying anymore` it was as if she was about to give away information that she had been instructed to keep to herself, and retreated to her desk in silence, where she began acting in an inconspicuous manner, by shuffling through the files and notes scattered about her desk.

The patients had been sedated so they would have a good night`s, rest, and the lighting in the ward had been lowered leaving the ward in semi darkness. This was to enable the patients to sleep and the nurses to see what they were doing if any of the patient needed help.

Meanwhile, Joan, had switched on the camera strapped to her head and proceeded to check every bed and corner of the ward, but saw nothing untoward, until Anne, moved silently to her side and taking her arm, she pointed to the shimmering figure of a nurse, who had suddenly appeared and was gently stroking each patient`s head, as she moved from one bed to another.

"Oh God, not her," Sister James whispered fearfully.

Joan, and Anne, watched the colour drain from the Sister`s face, as she sat clutching the sides of her desk, as a look of extreme dread contorted her features.

In an instant, Joan, aimed the camcorder she was holding directly towards the figure, then gasped when the apparition turned to expose her shattered features.

To her horror, Joan, saw that the woman's face was damaged almost beyond recognition. The shattered bones of her skull exposed the remaining pulverised grey matter of her brain, along with the shattered cheek bones, nose, jaw and splintered teeth, while the remaining eyeball dangling on her right cheek appeared to be looking directly at Joan.

Adding to her appallingly gruesome appearance, was the torn, filthy nurse's uniform that was soaked with huge spattering's of blood. Her stockings were ragged and ripped to shreds, exposing the bones of her bloodstained broken legs where her feet were stuck out at peculiar angles. But equally horrendous, was the bloody mangled mess of the stub of her lacerated arm that moved from just! above the elbow, as if the spirit believed it was still there, as she stroked each sleeping patients head.

For one sickening moment, Joan, felt her stomach heave, as the bile threatened to erupt from her stomach when feeling a sudden surge of nausea sweep through her as she stared in disbelief at the shattered flesh and tissue of the young woman's broken body.

"Oh my God!" Anne, gasped. "Mum!"

"Shush," Joan, whispered, not wanting to awaken any of the patients, as the disquieting figure carried on stroking and whispering comforting words to the sleeping patients.

The phantom figure then pulled herself upright, and after giving an inclination of satisfaction, she cast her gaze across the sleeping patients, then floated over to the medicine cabinet and disappeared.

"She believes that she is still alive," Joan whispered.

Nevertheless despite the ghastly appearance of the nurse, Joan felt a jolt of satisfaction pass through her.

At last she had the proof she needed of what she had been searching for over the years on camera. Proof that spirit can return to where it had been appreciated and loved, but most important, was that Joan had the proof she needed for the hospital committee, of what was causing fear amongst the patients and staff.

Anne, who was ashen but nevertheless filled with excitement, suggested to her mum that they should return to their quarters and examine the recording to ensure they had managed to catch the apparition on film.

"No," Joan, replied, "first we wait and see if anything else happens."

"But mum,"

"No, just sit down and be quiet and wait."

CHAPTER TWENTY FOUR

SUICIDE

Only a few minutes had passed after the appalling incident, when one of the women patients rose from her bed and padded softly across the bare wooden floor. It was obvious that she was in a state of somnambulism, as she unseeingly crossed the ward and walked slowly over to the door and opened it.

"Quick! switch on your camcorder and keep an eye on the ward," Joan, whispered to Anne, "I`ll follow the patient and find out what she does and where she goes."

For some unknown reason however, Sister James, who was seated at her desk didn't looked up as the woman left her bed, nor did she make a move to stop the patient from leaving the ward when she opened the door.

The woman left the ward with Joan following close behind and made her way to the outer door, that she unlocked and opened, then clad only in her nightdress and bare footed she walked out into the freezing cold snowstorm.

Joan immediately rushed forward to grab the woman and bring her back inside, but the woman turned with such a grotesque glare of malevolence on her face, that it caused Joan to stop and take a sharp intake of breath. The look of pure evil emanating from her eyes sent Joan reeling, while at the same time sending a sharp stab of terror into her heart that she had never experienced before.

"Oh may heaven protect us all," Joan, gasped. "The woman is possessed." The woman then let out an unearthly shriek and gave a furious roar of outrage before Joan, felt an invisible force of energy give her such an almighty push, sending her stumbling backwards into Anne, who had disregarded her mother`s words and had followed close behind. The intense power of the woman`s incredible strength, not only sent Joan reeling, but at the same instance Anne was also propelled down onto the cold wet ground.

Then, by the time they had regained their footing, the woman was moving at lightning speed towards the railway line, where a fast approaching Express was heading.

To their horror, they watched as she climbed onto the railway bridge and was standing on the slippery structure waving her arms into the air laughing and shouting. "I`m coming! I`m coming!"

"We`ve got to stop her!" Joan, yelled.

But her voice however, was lost beneath the thunderous roars of the howling wind and thunder. Together Joan, and Anne, raced towards the demented patient, where at times they found themselves slipping falling onto their backsides when their feet skidded away from beneath them. Then to Joan`s, dismay the moment she reached her` the woman leapt from the railway bridge into the front of the speeding locomotive.

"Oh God, no!" Joan shrieked when hearing the squeal of brakes as the driver attempted to halt the speeding train. But it was too late, the fall from the height of the bridge was enough to seriously injure or kill anyone, or the electric line would have done so, and no one could have survived the impact and momentum of the speeding Express train.

CHAPTER TWENTY FIVE

POLICE ENQUIRY

It had taken until after lunch time the following day for the police to finish questioning everyone who had any connection with the asylum. This included nurses, two non-resident doctors who were called in for emergencies, cleaners and caretakers.

There had been no visitors at the time of the incident, to be honest, the patients never had any visitors. Matron had to explain to the police however, that the patients came from well-known society people and were an embarrassment to them. Therefore, as they would have been an embarrassment to the elite families, they had been transferred as far away as possible from them, to be hidden away and forgotten.

Nevertheless, despite refusing the offers of comfort from the police, Joan, and Anne, who had been left traumatised after witnessing the suicide, sat silent and subdued in their room, until Anne, broke the disquieting silence.

"Do you think we should go home?" she asked in a demoralised tone.

"What!"

"I said, do you think we should pack up and go home?

"Joan, stared at her in surprise by her unanticipated question. "No, just give me time to get my head together, I hope you realise just how big a shock this has been to me, by being unable to save her. "Oh heaven help me I couldn't stop her!" she sobbed covering her face with both hands. "I'd almost reached her when she jumped, dear God, I will never forget the look on that poor train driver`s face after he had stopped the train and run down the track, praying to God that his train hadn`t hit her. "Joan, held her hands up in a helpless gesture as tears poured down her face. "I wish I had never scrambled down that slope to help, I will never forget the sight of the poor woman`s severed and mangled body, crushed to a pulp beneath the wheels of that engine. Joan, hunched herself into a ball sobbing even harder.

"Oh mum, it wasn't your fault," Anne, placed a comforting arm around her mother`s heaving shoulders. "It would have happened no matter what! you were just the unlucky person being there at that time."

"You're a good girl," Joan, acknowledged wiping the tears from her eyes and she patted her daughter`s hand as she rose to her feet.

"I know," Anne replied with a cheeky grin. "What about us taking a walk to the staff canteen and having a cuppa? Maybe talking to someone will help take your mind off what happened?"

"You`re right," Joan, stood up and blew her nose, then went over to the sink to rinse her red` rimmed swollen eyes with cold water. "Sitting here moping isn't doing any good, it won`t bring her back will it? I hope the cold water has taken the swelling down," she murmured, as she walked past the mirror, then cringed when seeing her swollen nose and the puffy, red blotches on her face reflecting back at her.

"Don`t worry about it, mum, you look fine, just act natural, if you can!" Anne, couldn't help but smirk at her own witticism.

Joan, threw her a scathing look, "Come on cheeky let`s have that tea." As they made their way to the canteen, Anne, suggested that it might be a good idea for them to take a break and rest for the day. Then if she was feeling any better, she might be up to investigating the Men`s ward that night. "You never know mum the phantom nurse might put in an appearance there.

"Oh yes," Joan retorted, more harshly than she meant to. "And witness some other poor sod leave the ward to jump of the bridge and go under a train."

Anne, suddenly realised what she had said and quickly apologised. "I'm sorry mum, as I suggested earlier, perhaps it would be better if we went back to our room and packed our bags and left. After all, we now have the proof that the Trustees were asking for haven't we?"

"I don't know," Joan, answered thoughtfully. "I don't think running away would solve the problem would it? Maybe she only puts in an appearance at night, when one of the patients is about to kill themselves."

"Mum," Anne, interrupted. "You know that ghosts don't always wait until night to put in an appearance, they can crop up anytime they wish, and the person involved does not have to be thinking of killing themselves."

Joan gazed quizzically at her daughter. "Go on, what are you trying to say?

"If you recall," Anne, began to enlighten her mother, "it was 9am on a sunny Saturday morning when we saw the apparition of a motor bike rider dressed in his leathers, he was holding a crash helmet in his hands, and was standing outside a row of houses near the traffic lights. That was when we were driving to Barnsley market, while we were waiting for the lights to change, he looked at us then disappeared through the wall of one of the houses nearby."

Joan, hesitated and thought for a moment, "You're right," she said, "I remember now, he looked fairly young didn't he? I'm sorry love I'm not thinking straight, come on let's get that cup of tea and something to eat, I can always think better on a full stomach."

"Huh, tell me about it," Anne, said rolling her eyes as she pushed open the canteen door.

CHAPTER TWENTY SIX

UNDERSTANDING

Although Anne, was putting on a brave face for her mother's sake, she feeling subdued and low when she went over to the metal urn and filled a large teapot with boiling hot water. As if on automatic pilot, she next picked up two mugs and returned to the table and placed two Camomile tea bags they had brought with them into the pot and waited. While in muted silence, her mum went over to the breakfast bar and picked up two plates of toast and jam then set them down on the table when she returned.

Joan, however was feeling equally emotional, she couldn't clear her mind from the previous night's events and was unable to eat anything and pushed her plate away.

To their surprise however, while they were seated at the table, two of the nurses came over to Joan, and congratulated her on the way she had tried to save the patient.

"I'm Mavis, Nurse Morris, and this is Paula, Nurse Simpson" Mavis said, introducing them both."

"Edna has always had a problem with her sleep walking," Paula informed them. "She was always seeing things as well," commented a nurse from a nearby table.

"Yes" Nurse James, piped up who was drinking her tea, then a look of nervousness flitted across her face when she glanced over to the closed door as if expecting the Matron to appear at any time.

"She said it was as if the devil trying to get inside her head," she commented lowering her voice.

Joan, suddenly felt a flutter of unease race through her when recalling the malevolent look on Edna`s, face when she pushed her to the ground. "Did she ever mention a nurse stroking her head?" Joan, asked.

"Yes she did," Nurse Davies, replied, as she joined them at the table. "Other patients have seen her as-well, even the male patients in the other ward say they have watched her go around at night, stopping by those who were restless and stroking their heads until they became calm."

"That's right," another chorused. "I didn't dare enter the ward one night, I had just opened the ward door and was about to go in, when I saw her standing over a patient stroking his head, I was so scared that I turned and ran to tell the Matron."

Joan, gave a sigh when already knowing what the Matron`s reaction would be, nevertheless she asked, "What did she say."

" She told me not to be so stupid, and that the silly rumours about the phantom nurses was affecting my better judgment. She then instructed me in no uncertain terms to get on with the work that I was being paid to do and left it at that," the nurse remarked huffily.

Joan, glanced about at the worried faces as they watched and waited for an explanation as to why a number of nurses were haunting the wards. "Can anyone tell me the name of the nurses who haunts the wards?" she asked in the hope of getting a rational account from the worried nurses

"Which nurse? there are several of them that have been seen moving about the wards," Mavis replied.

"The one who is badly scarred, can any one of you tell me who she is?." Joan asked. "That would have to be Nurse Ruth Tennant," Sister Sanderson, interjected. "She always made sure that the patients were comfortable at night, she used to go around singing lullabies and stroking their heads to put them to sleep, they loved her for it. But for some unknown reason however, one day after a row with Matron she became distressed and raced out of the hospital. She climbed onto the bridge then threw herself down onto the electrified rail track in front of the approaching Express train, she didn't stand a chance of surviving that."

CHAPTER TWENTY SEVEN

BARBARIC TREATMENT

Joan acknowledged what Sister Sanderson was saying. "So that is the reason why she appeared so badly injured! she must be the one whom we caught on tape."

"You did?" Nurse Morris`s, shocked voice rang around the silent canteen.

"Yes I did," Joan, replied.

Before Joan, could add any more, Sister Darwin interrupted. "There is something else, please don`t let the Matron know that I have told you this, but no one is allowed to go into the lower part of the hospital, the door leading down is always kept locked and matron has the keys."

"That`s right," a mumble of voice harmonized about the room.

"Some years ago, Sister Darwin, began, a group of nurses were told by a man who used to work here, that the door leads down to the old disused operating theatres and the padded cells. But that's not all," she continued. "We heard that in the past electronic treatment and lobotomies were carried out in those operating theatres."

"Yes and other cruel experiments were performed on the helpless victims," Nurse Morris added. "They were bloody heartless creatures those doctors."

A murmur of agreement rose from the nurses.

"What`s a lobotomy?" Anne, asked, eager to learn more of the hospital`s abominable research.

"A lobotomy is where they used a sharp pointed instrument, something like an ice pick, that they hammered into the front of the patient's skull, just under the eyelid, then they cut the nerves in the brain that connect the cortex to the thalamus. It was supposed to calm the patient," Sister Darwin explained.

Anne, sat back in shock, grateful that she was sitting down or she would have fallen. "You have to be joking," she gasped.

"No I'm not," Sister Darwin replied. "They also pulled out patient's rotten teeth and removed body parts, believing that infection was the cause of madness. Patients were also place in ice cold water baths thinking that the freezing cold water would shock them back to sanity. But the shock of being immersed in freezing cold water killed some of the patients. Not only were they allowed to carry out these procedures in the name of science, but sadistic and cruel acts and ECT treatment also took place. In some cases, when carrying out ECT it took five strong men to hold a patient down, one to secure a firm hold on the head, two to hold the arms and two the legs, as they convulsed."

"Some of those poor souls ended up with disjointed hips and spinal injuries and were crippled for life. This was due to the pressure required of holding them down' other patients who underwent the treatments that were forced upon them, ended up unable to connect with the living world anymore. In fact some of them, after the treatments ended up brain dead or zombified. In my opinion it was the ones who died who were the lucky ones, even then their deaths were fabricated lies, when they were recorded as pneumonia."

"*Bloody Hell*," Joan, cursed under her breath.

The unexpected statement by the sister sent shock waves reeling even amongst the staff. They had never heard of the hospital's past hair' raising history, nor of what had occurred there over the years.

"Oh yes," Paula Sanderson, expressed grimly. "Nothing was ever said about the poor service men who arrived here suffering from shell shock during both World Wars."

CHAPTER TWENTY EIGHT

CHAOS IN THE CANTEEN

"Has the heating gone off?" Nurse Williams asked, rubbing her bare arms to improve the circulation.

"No, the radiators are red hot," Paula, replied, placing her hand on the metal heater, then snatched it away when feeling the scorching hot heat.

Within seconds however, after Paula, had mentioned the wounded and dying servicemen, the temperature in the canteen began to drop even lower. And the three, fluorescent lights suspended by chains from the ceiling, began swinging wildly, before eventually flickering and dying out leaving the canteen in semi darkness, and the eerie sound of muffled footsteps, shuffling about the exterior of the canteen.

"Oh my God! one of the nurses cried, making a mad dash for the door, but before she could reached it, the door slammed shut in front of her locking itself securely. "Let me out! Let me out!" she screamed frantically, pulling at the door handle, but the door refused to budge, then when she comprehended that it was something beyond her understanding, she collapsed in a heap onto the floor. In the meantime, the rest of the medical staff, who were too afraid to help her, stepped back unsure of what to do and huddled close to one another.

"Joan, what do we do?" someone called, in a voice filled with a mixture of confusion and fear.

"Believe me, when I say that you are all safe," Joan raised her voice, so everyone could hear her above the harrowing sounds of the terrified women. "Please listen, situations like this have happened to me on many occasions, and when they did, no one was hurt." "I know it won`t be easy, but I just want everyone to stay calm and try not to show any sign of fear. If it is any of the servicemen or a patient who has died here, then they are just trying to make their presence known. Now please, please try to understand that you are not in any danger, believe me you are not in any danger." Directly as Joan, referred to the servicemen, the lights resumed their normal brightness and ceased to swing and the heat began rising to its normal temperature.

"Thank goodness," someone whispered softly amongst the murmuring voices. "I told you, that, whoever was here had no intention of harming any of you, now please calm down and return to your seats."

A number of nurses gave the excuse that they should get back to the wards, while the rest of them resumed their seats. However, when Joan, glanced at the worried faces watching her, she smiled to herself when noticing that most of the staff were seated together instead of sitting at separated tables.

CHAPTER TWENTY NINE

JOAN'S EXPLANATION

"Now that everyone has calmed down, could I please have your attention? I have something to tell you," Joan, declared confidently. The hush in the canteen, however, was broken when an array of anxious voices began bombarding Joan, with questions. "Please. Please be quiet," she called, standing up and holding out her hands for silence.

"I will answer your questions later, but first I feel that it is imperative that you listen to what I have to tell you." After a few disquieting mumbles from the staff, who had stayed after the bizarre occurrences Joan began to explain what she had witnessed in the Women's ward, and that she had caught the disfigured apparition of Ruth Tennant on film.

"You have?" Nurse Morris gasped, with a hint of disbelief in her voice, and leapt to her feet, and grasped the back of a chair so hard that her knuckles turned white.

"Yes I am sorry to say this, but now I understand what happened to her, so if you will please sit down, I will clarify what I have filmed."

Nurse Morris, resumed her seat and began clutching her apron and twisting it, to relieve the tension inside of her.

"What I have on film is not a pretty sight," Joan, began. "Ruth's, face and body was badly mutilated and the bones of her shattered remains were exposed."

"You have this on film?" Sister Sanderson asked with sense of incredibility in her tone. "Yes," Joan, acknowledged her question. "Most of her clothing was torn and soaked with her blood and it was evident that she had been dragged violently across rough ground."

"Oh dear God no," nurse Morris, moaned. "She was such a caring person, but you are right, it would have been Ruth, she must have been the one who frightened Edna, the other night."

"Yes and Ivy," Sister Sanderson added.

An uneasy hush descended about the room, until Anne, broke the tension, by asking if there had been any other sightings. Had there been any unusual sounds or occurrences reported in any other part of the hospital, especially the abandoned area in particular?"

"We wouldn't know," Sister Darwin, replied, rising unsteadily to her feet and holding onto the chair back for support.

"We are forbidden to go to any other floor than the ground floor, anyway everything is fastened of so we have to stay on the ground floor."

"And we have strict orders that no one is allowed to go through that door," Mavis, added pointing towards the door concealed by the screen. "Matron is the only one holding the key, so we can`t go through there."

"Why ever not?" Joan, asked, knowing what it would be like through there.

"Matron said that it was too dark, and maybe dangerous if we entered the corridor."

"Have any of you been in the corridor?" Anne, enquired.

No, they replied, shaking their heads.

Joan, gave a deep sigh of frustration, she had been hoping to find answers to some of the questions that she desperately needed answering. Then a thought came to her, "I think I know the reason for the hauntings, I believe it is connected to the Mat—"

Joan, stopped herself from what she was about to say, when the door was flung open and the red` faced, blustering Matron entered the canteen.

"You were saying the Matron is what?" she commented tartly, throwing an acid glare at Joan, then spun round, glaring at everyone in the dining room. No one spoke.

"I think it is about time you people stopped gossiping and got back to work?" she announced curtly. "There are patients who need looking after, and you two?" she snapped, throwing a derogatory glare at Joan, and Anne. Then as if having a second thought she spun on her heels and marched off behind the nurses, as they hastily fled from the canteen.

"She is one hell of a nasty bitch!" Anne, retorted, shaking her head, "I can`t understand why she is so much against us trying to help."

Joan gave her a knowing look, "Don`t worry too much about it," she said. "I think I may have the answer."

CHAPTER THIRTY

APPARITION IN THEIR ROOM

"Do you think we should check out the attic?" Joan, posed the question to Anne, as they entered the canteen the following day for breakfast, then stopped what she, was about to say when noticing that Anne, was acting in a strange manner. "Have I said something wrong?" she asked.

"No, let`s get our breakfast then I will tell you," Anne, replied in a sombre tone, as they entered the canteen. Concerned by her daughter`s strange behaviour, Joan, chose a table away from prying ears when sensing that something was wrong, before asking Anne what was troubling her.

"Oh it`s nothing to worry about," Anne replied, putting her head down and becoming silent. "Anne will you please tell me what it is? Maybe I can help?.."

Anne, gave a reluctant sigh and shuffled in her seat. "I didn't like to say anything about it before," she said raising her head. "But ever since we arrived, I have felt that someone was watching us in our room."

"Oh," Joan responded in a cautious tone, "Yes, I must admit that I`ve also felt it."

"What!" Anne exclaimed loudly, causing the staff to look their way, "why didn't you tell me?"

"Because I didn't want to alarm you, I know what you can be like at times."

"Oh for goodness` sake mother!" Anne, snapped letting out a groan of frustration. "I`m not a bloody child who is afraid of its own shadow."

"I`m sorry love, I didn`t mean anything wrong, it`s just that----"

"Never mind, I understand, now can I finish what I was about to tell you. "Joan nodded her head, as she waited for Anne to disclose what the problem was.

"Right then," she began, "every night at around midnight, I have been woken by someone touching me! at first I thought it was you, but when I looked to see who it was, no one was there. Then when I glanced over to your bed, in the darkness I could just make out the silhouette of a man bending over you. I don't know who he was, but when I called out and switched on my bedside lamp, he disappeared."

Joan, became instantly alert. "Why didn't you wake me?" she asked sharply, irritated by her daughter keeping silent regarding the spectral figure.

"Because I didn't want to upset you," Anne replied, fighting to keep her temper under control.

"Oh I`m sorry love," Joan, reached across the table and took Anne`s hand in hers. "I really am sorry, I didn`t mean to snap at you, but whatever`s happening here is starting to get to me, to be honest it`s affecting everyone in the hospital, staff and patients alike."

"I know mum," Anne, murmured, glancing furtively about the canteen. "No one is immune to the phenomena, something strange is happening wherever we go here. I think" Anne, then stopped for a moment, as if giving thought at what she was about to say, when she was distracted by her mum asking something.

"Can you remember what the man looked like, or what he was wearing?" "Hell mum, you've made me forget what I was about to say," Anne, retorted angrily. "And yes, I can remember what he looked like, but the only time I saw him clearly was one night when the moon was shining brightly and it lit up our room. It was only a vague sighting though, as I could only see him from behind, but I don`t think he was old, as he had dark hair, and was wearing a white coat like the doctor`s wear."

"That`s odd," her mother replied. "Because that is what I`ve seen bending over you at night. Anne, felt her skin crawl. "Mum, can we change the subject and concentrate on something else before I go stark staring bonkers` all this is starting to get to me, she said, giving a shudder.

CHAPTER THIRTY ONE

KEYS TO THE ATTIC

"Mum?"

"What?"

"Who, or what, do you think is causing the hauntings?"

"I'm only guessing," Joan, replied, lowering her voice and glancing about the canteen to ensure no-one would hear what she was about to say. I think the Matron is somehow connected to the suicides, deaths and hauntings that are occurring here."

"You do," Anne, replied in awe, amazed by her mother's unexpected revelation. "Now that you have said that, I think that I'm beginning to understand what is happening here." Anne, said reaching across the table and taking hold of Joan's hand. "Mum I know this is changing the focus of what you have just told me, but I was wondering, do you recall seeing that there was a steel, barred gate, fitted with a heavy padlock and chain barring the stairs leading up to the attic?"

"Yes, what about it?"

"Well we couldn't go any further could we?"

"That's right, why do you ask?"

"Well, I believe there is a strong possibility that the locked door leading into the attic holds the answer to everything that is occurring here."

"Clever girl, I never thought of that," Joan, remarked thoughtfully. "I've so much going off in my mind at the moment, that I can hardly think straight, but you can bet that bloody Matron will most likely have the keys for both the gate and the door. Come on," she said determinedly, "let's get those keys."

They hurried to the Matron's office where they found her sitting at her desk and she grimaced at them as they entered. "What do you want," she snarled obviously peeved by the intrusion, whereby Joan, asked her politely for the keys to the attic. "You can't have them." she snapped, you were asked to investigate the wards and nothing more."

"That is where you're wrong," Joan, retorted angrily standing her ground. "I can contact the Trustees right now and inform them that you are unwilling to co-operate in my investigation, if that's what you want?" Joan watched as the Matron's face turned a deep crimson.

"Here" she snarled! Taking a bunch of keys from the drawer of her desk and slamming them down onto the leather surface. "Take them! If you are as clever as you say you are, then find out for yourselves what the others are for. Now get out of my office," she shouted. With a calculative movement, Joan reached over and scouped up the keys from the desk and pushed them into her pocket, before the Matron had the opportunity to change her mind, then calmly left the office.

The Matron's cynical attitude towards them opening the door to the attic, had caused Joan to become concerned at what she would probably find there. Nevertheless, Joan, and Anne, set about following the diagram the Matron had given them earlier.

They were however, wary of using the rickety staircase they had previously climbed, to gain access to the first floor. Whereby Anne suggested that they take a look at the door that was fitted in the hoarding at the foot of the main staircase, that had been placed there to stop the patients from wandering up the stairs and meandering around in the upstairs wards. By a stroke of luck however, Joan, found that one of the keys from the bunch, fitted and unlocked the door in the hoarding, thus giving them easy access to the main staircase.

"What do you say to us going up there?" she asked taking a swift glance around the entrance hall and reception area to ensure no one was watching them.

"It`s alright with me," Anne replied enthusiastically` she was eager at the prospect of reaching the attic on the main staircase, rather than risk the dangerous one they had climbed previously.

To be on the safe side, they paused for a moment before unlocking and opening the creaking door before entering, and glanced around the area to ensure there was no one walking about or watching them in the near vicinity. "It`s clear come on" Anne whispered furtively, then giving each other a smile of encouragement, they entered and locked the door behind them.

CHAPTER THIRTY TWO

THE STAIRCASE

"My goodness," Joan whispered softly, when using the full beam of their torches to light up the staircase, and were astounded to find that it was carpeted, and the whole area was clean, with not a speck of dust in sight. The day previously, they had been in such a hurry to escape from the terrifying phenomena, that they hadn`t noticed if the stairs were clean or dirty. Their full concentration had been on getting to fundamental safety and they had also managed to get through the hoarding door without a key.

"Anne, this staircase looks as if it is used on a regular basis? I don`t know by who, but something doesn't sit right here," Joan murmured quietly, as she shone her torch in every direction above and about the surrounding area. "Have you noticed there isn`t any dust, or cobwebs? nor is there any sign of rodents! In fact, this staircase appears to have been cleaned recently` look at the carpet it`s spotless! It also appears to be the original carpet from the last owner of The Grange.

"You could be right mum! And the banister rail has been polished," Anne remarked, running her fingers along the smooth shining surface of the mahogany wood.

"Stop." Joan hissed. Anne froze, "What is it?" she responded quickly.

"Stay where you are. I don`t think we should go any further somethings not right."

"What do you mean not right?"

"I don`t quite know," Joan replied, with a hint of uncertainty in her voice, "but something doesn't add up here, it`s too easy! There was no one on duty at the reception desk and we both know that there is always someone there in the daytime, and someone would have stopped us from opening that door at the bottom of the stairs. No, I feel something is wrong ."

"Do you think the Matron knew that we would be asking to come up here today?" Anne asked, in a voice filled with concern. "If so then I think she`s up to mischief, and if she is, then I suggest that we carry on with the investigation and not be put off by that rotten old windbag?"

Joan had to supress a laugh, Anne had never been a person to mince words and was often in trouble for speaking her mind, nevertheless she was in agreement with her there.

"You`re right," Joan shone her torch further up the staircase towards the balcony above, before seeing a landing then more stairs leading up onto the balcony. "Let`s get onto that landing before we make up our minds what we should do."

It was still fresh in Joan`s mind what had happened previously on the second floor and she didn't want the same thing occurring again. Switch on your head camera and I`ll use the camcorder, if there is anything up there that we see or feel is dangerous, we go back, if that's alright with you?"

Anne gave a nod of assent.

Cautiously, they climbed the rest of the stairs without any incident until reaching the landing, then moved up onto the first floor balcony, then up the stairs of the second floor balcony.

But immediately they stepped onto the bare timbers of the balcony, they became aware that the floor boards beneath their feet were slightly unstable. The boards sagged in places, and were bending, and groaning beneath the pressure of their combined weight, To make matters worse was the discovery that the floor was buried beneath polluted vermin droppings, skeletal bones and remains of small creatures, and huge chunks of plaster. The complete area was exactly the same as they had discovered in their previous investigation.

Shining their lamps about the decrepit area, they noticed that cobwebs had formed their own constructive barriers, that wove amid each gap of the once vibrant balustrade. This was now infected with a collection of disease riddled insect infestation, buried deep inside the thick webbing. The parasites had constructed their nests to lay their eggs and had lain there, undisturbed for years.

"Mum look! Over there!" Anne motioned with her torch, "I just turned to the zenith level on my torch for extra light to enable me to see further along the balcony and what did I find? We never noticed with it being so dark, that the balcony ran all the way round the hospital. And isn`t that the area where we carried out our investigation the other day and experienced that dreadful phenomenon? If so, then we must be at the opposite side of the hospital above the men`s wards.

Joan accelerated the light on her torch and swung the powerful beam across the landing to where Anne was indicating. "Good grief! You are right," Joan exclaimed, as she scanned the desolate area through the dense intertwined mass of cobwebs, reaching from the ceiling and criss-crossing the passages almost to the floor.

"We didn't come up the main staircase, we entered the balcony from the servants` staircase, on the opposite side, if so!" "We are! We must be! You`re right!" Joan exclaimed excitedly. We are on the opposite side of the hospital, and we haven't checked this side yet. Hell! in all that panic to escape the other day, we didn't stop to think did we? We just ran."

At that moment, Joan, and Anne, weren't aware of the several groups of phantom servicemen watching them` their minds at that moment, were overwhelmed by locating the unexplored area of the Grange.

CHAPTER THIRTY THREE

GHOSTS

"Why the Dickins couldn't they have switched the electricity on? It`s so dark in here," Anne, complained rubbing her eyes on her sleeve, after staring for such a long length of time into the obscure murky darkness, until her eyes felt as if they were filled with grit. " I`m sick and tired of being unable to see where I`m treading, and goodness only knows what keeps touching my face`."

"I know what you mean," Joan replied when feeling and hearing the vermin`s skeletal remains of unidentifiable creatures crunching beneath her feet. "And yes I agree with you, I wish there was more, light up here, I`m tired of worrying about where I`m putting my feet."

Together they moved cautiously forward, where both noticed in the menacing stillness, that four of the disused wards had wide open doors, and as they drew closer, they could see that there was a single ray of subdued light emanating from each of the wards.

"Get behind me, if anything nasty should happen then forget about me and run, save yourself," Joan whispered, keeping her voice low so as not to alert anyone waiting in the shadows.

"You have to be joking,"

"No I`m not."

"Blood hell mam, I`m not leaving you."

"Anne, for once in your life do as you are told."

"Forget about it, mum, were staying together."

"You are a stubborn little bugger," Joan, hissed. Nevertheless she was proud of her daughter's consideration in opting to stay with her. "Are you ready?" she asked.

"Yes."

"Right here we go." Joan, guardedly entered the room, closely followed by Anne, where they observed that every window was obscured by strong wire mesh and metal bars, identical to what they had seen in the ward's opposite.

Thick layers of dust, grime and cobwebs were entwined throughout the mesh, along with ivy that had wrapped it's chocking tendrils around the outer bars and were preventing the full strength of the sun's diminishing winter rays of light to penetrate through the filthy glass.

"My God, it is more like a prison than a hospital," Joan, murmured softly, as they made their way from ward to ward. The daunting sight of the long dark corridors exiting from the balcony and dividing the eight sets of rooms running the entire length of the building, were enough to give a living soul a permanent nightmare.

"Mum?"

"What?"

"Did you see the weird subdued glimmer in that corridor over there?"

"No, I didn't," Joan, replied, shining her torch into the black, empty space, but couldn't see anything amiss.

"Are you certain? " Anne, asked, then stopped, when feeling the hairs on the back of her neck beginning to prickle. "Oh my God!" she whispered, when sensing that someone was standing very close to her, and knew it wasn't her mother, as Joan, was already scouting ahead, so it could only mean one thing.

"Mum! she shrieked, then froze` not daring to move.

"What now?" Joan, snapped, turning to shine the light in Anne's direction, then almost lost the grip on her torch, when observing, four ghostly entities of servicemen in full military uniform, surrounded by a bizarre dull grey light, were standing strategically positioned beside Anne.

"Mum," Anne, quivered, staring at her mother and not daring to glance at what was alongside her.

"It`s alright Anne," Joan, spoke in an assertive tone. "Stay where you are, they won`t harm you."

Even though Joan, was feeling slightly unnerved, she turned her gaze to the phantom entities, and explained to them that she was there to help release their earth bound spirits, and get them to, the higher side of life. In a flash of understanding, the men nodded in her direction and the group evaporated into the shadows. "It`s alright they`re gone there`s nothing to worry about," Joan whispered, taking her trembling daughter in her arms, nothing is going to hurt you."

Nevertheless it took a few moments for Anne, to regain her self-restraint , before allowing her mother to release her, and followed her further into the sorrowful depressing surroundings of the oppressive building.

"I didn't want to come up here again," Anne, grumbled, shining her torch about the gloomy, depressing ward, dreading what she might see next, and observing the discarded medical equipment propped against the walls and laying scattered about the bug` riddled floor.

"Anything could happen and nobody would find us until it was too late," she grumbled. "Then we would end up like the things we have come here to study."

"Shut up and stop griping," Joan snapped, as she concentrated on filming the obsolete equipment scattered about the floor and walls.

Despite the irritation she was feeling, Anne, held back the retort she was about to make. Joan, however knew that Anne, was worried and stopped filming to give her a few words of encouragement. But at that moment Anne, was struck dumb, when the light from her mother`s torch fell upon a nurse who was standing with her back towards them.

"Oh shit," Anne, whispered grabbing hold of her mother`s arm, then screamed, when instead of it being her mother, she felt bones and wrinkled cold skin beneath her fingers.

"Mum!" she shrieked in terror, and fearfully shone her light onto what she was touching. The moment she did however, Anne found herself petrified with fear and unable to move, when finding herself face to face with an intimidating old crone with long straggly grey hair. Most of the sickening spectre`s teeth were missing from the gaping black hole of its mouth, from where a foul, rank stink was emanating directly into Anne` face

"Mum!" she yelled again, but Joan, who was getting annoyed with Anne`s irrational behaviour ignored her and carried on with what she was doing. Leaving Anne, to stare, as the deplorable skeletal corpse gave an unnatural cackling chortle then faded away into the darkness.

CHAPTER THIRTY FOUR

DID YOU SEE HER

"That`s it! I`ve had enough," Anne screamed, "I`m leaving, I`m getting out of here. "In her haste to get away, in the darkness, Anne, charged into a number of empty metal gas and oxygen cylinders that had been left precariously propped against the wall, that fell to the floor with an almighty crash along with Anne.

Joan, spun round in alarm at the unexpected racket, when the din made by the cylinders rolling and clattering against one another sent reverberating echoes abounding throughout the entire second floor.

The pandemonium was deafening in the cold, eerie, abandoned space, where Anne, lay on the rodent` infested floor in intrepid fear, not daring to move.

"Mum, mum," she whispered as loudly as she dared, not wanting anything other than her mother to hear her. "I want to leave, I can`t stand anymore! I`ve had enough!" she cried.

"Oh for goodness` sake, we`ve only just got started`" she heard her mother say. "Anyway what the dickens are you doing on the floor? Get up you idiot."

"I tripped over this bloody rubbish trying to get away from that old woman," she fumed, rolling onto her side then clambered to her feet. "Didn't you see her?"

"See who?"

"That bloody old woman."

"What bloody old woman?"

106

"Oh forget it! Can`t we go back to our quarters? At least there`s some light in there?"

"No we can`t."

"Why not?"

"Because I say so

"But."

"No buts, just you listen to me, it took me ages to get permission from the people running this place to investigate the hauntings, and to allow us to spend a full week here.

Currently the law states they can`t sell the property and land, unless it is disclosed that it is viable.

"Well I think it should have been closed down with the rest of the hospital."

"Oh shut up and stop moaning, you`re starting to sound like your dad`s mother."

"That is below the belt," Anne snapped.

"Well if the shoe fits` wear it."

"Listen! What was that.?"

I don`t know," Anne replied hesitantly, "you go look, I`ll stay here."

"What on your own?"

Anne glanced around the dismal surroundings and shuddered at the thought of what could be waiting to grab her, within seconds she felt her bravado diminish. "Wait!" she yelled watching her mother`s light disappear into the dark confines of the doorway. "Don`t leave me! I`m coming with you." she screeched, when hearing the squeaking rodents gathering around her, just waiting to gnaw at her body if she fell again.

CHAPTER THIRTY FIVE

JACK ELLIOT CARTAKER

Grouchy and wittering non-stop, Anne, chased after her mother, terrified at the thought of being left alone in the creepy haunted room with its ghosts and rats, which gave her the creeps. She hurried after her mother, who was making her way towards the ward from where the weird sounds were emanating, calling to her to not enter the room.

"For goodness` sake, stop whinging will you," Joan hissed, turning towards her daughter, then almost fell when she tripped and staggered forward over something lying at her feet. "What on earth?" she exclaimed, shining the light down onto the floor.

"Mother!" Anne, gasped, "it looks like soiled bed linen that someone`s thrown down, but it wasn't here when we came along this corridor earlier."

"You`re right, it wasn't," Joan, replied, directing her flashlight about the surrounding area, but there was nothing to be seen. She then pushed Anne, behind her as she observed a strong beam of light from a lamp heading towards them. "Get behind me and stay there," Joan hissed, as she waited anxiously for whoever it was to approach nearer. "Don't come any closer` I warn you," Joan, called as loud as she could. "I`m armed," she lied.

"It`s alright, it`s only me, Jack Elliot the caretaker," a voice called from out of the darkness."

I patrol these corridors every hour in the evening and night, until Harry, takes over the day shift, he called in and asked me to do his shift, he wasn't feeling too good. Didn't the Matron tell you back there?"

"No`" Joan, replied, shaking her head and giving a sigh of relief when hearing Harry`s name mentioned.

"That sour` face old bag wouldn't let on nothing unless she was ordered to," he muttered begrudgingly. "Nobody likes her you know."

"Yes and I can understand why" Joan, replied with a hint of sarcasm.

"You`re the ghost hunters, aren`t you?" he asked, peering closely at Joan, then at Anne.

"Yes, we are," Joan, replied.

"Well I can tell you this," he stated, wagging a grubby finger at them. "The worst hauntings at this hospital are down below in the basement, where the old operating theatres, the experimental wards and padded cells are. But I wouldn't advise you not to go there," he warned.

Joan, and Anne, looked at one other. "Operating theatres, Anne, uttered in an incredulous tone, so it is true they did experiment on helpless people?" She was so angry and repulsed at the idea of anyone being experimented on in the name of medical progress. She began cursing silently.

Jacks voice however was bitter when he, spoke of what had occurred there in the past. "Them poor buggers couldn't fight back, could they. They`d been drugged up to the eyeballs until there was no fight left in them. They were completely controlled by the Frankenstein medical bastards, who experimented on their brains and ended up crippling some and turned others into Zombies. Them that died were lucky, the poor sods. Then the, buggers had a hey day with the men coming here during the war suffering from shell shock, and the injuries they suffered, from the atrocities that went on in both wars.

"Oh! Oh!" he declared, when the beeper suddenly sounded on his belt. "I`d better be off before I get into bother with Matron. It`s time they retired that old bitch," he muttered grumpily. "But I honestly don`t believe that they can get anybody to replace her," he chuntered, throwing a worried glance behind himself. "She`s got ears and eyes up her bloody arse that woman, he then turned and walked away, sweeping his light into each empty ward before disappearing from sight as he rounded the bend of the next corridor, leaving Joan, and Anne, dumbfounded.

CHAPTER THIRTY SIX

THE STAIRCASE

Joan, had noticed the uneasy tension in her daughter, so to relax the situation, she suggested that they should return to their quarters, where they would have a hot drink and get warm. "Thanks mum, I`m freezing," Anne replied, trembling not just from the trauma of what was happening, but from the harsh cold that was stiffening her aching limbs.

Nevertheless, Anne`s nerves were shredded, and she hung onto her mother`s arm tightly, as they made their way through the dark, dingy corridors. Then using their head-lights to see straight ahead, they swung their torches from side to side to see if there was anything loitering in the shadows and they didn't stop until they had reached the balcony. When Joan, suddenly slithered to a halt, while at the same time grabbing hold of Anne, to stop her from moving any further forward, she had seen the spectral figure of an airman appear from out of the dark shadows, who was floating above the ground and heading straight towards them.

"Shush` don`t make a sound, stay exactly where you are," Joan whispered, when feeling Anne, stiffen, and watched as the phantom figure drew steadily closer.

"Blood hell mam! if the basement is worse than this, and like Jack Elliot said, then I don`t want to go anywhere near it," she stammered anxiously.

"Shush," Joan, whispered to her daughter, while at the same time keeping a watchful eye on the approaching apparition, "There has to be a reasonable explanation for this to be happening. They were however unable to prevent a gasp of shock from escaping their lips when they perceived his appearance. His face and body was damaged beyond recognition, but much worse was the stench of burnt flesh accompanying him. What Joan, found perplexing, was that his clothing and flying boots were undamaged, therefore it was obvious that he wanted them to see that he had been an RAF pilot.

The next thing Joan, felt however, was a weakening paralysis begin to sweep through her, and within seconds she was totally powerless to protect herself or her daughter from whatever was controlling her.

Anne, though had grasped the severity of the situation and pulled herself together. She grabbed hold of her mother by the shoulders and shook her until feeling a response. Then together, they watched as the spectral airman glid silently past them, along the balcony and disappeared through the wall of one of the empty wards.

"Mum, I feel sick," Anne groaned, holding her aching stomach. Then before Joan, could utter a word Anne was violently ill. Within seconds the rats and vermin were fighting one another to gobble up the nauseating contents of Anne`s last meal.

Come on, Joan, whispered urgently. "We`ve got to get out of here." Gently guiding Anne by the arm, Joan hurried her along the balcony, then down the wide staircase and out through the wooden door leading into the dimly lit entrance hall. "Thank goodness were out of there," Joan said as they both stood leaning against the wall panting and gasping for breath. Then Anne, asked the definitive question.

"Mum, did you notice there was no carpet on the staircase and it was filthy?"

CHAPTER THIRTY SEVEN

THE TELEPHONE CALL

"Mum?

""What?"

"Have you rung dad?"

"Anne, it is only six am."

"Oh! Well don`t forget to call him will you?"

"For goodness` Anne, sake, he will be asleep."

"No he won`t."

"He will."

"He won`t, he will be getting ready to go down to the yard."

"Mum!"

"What now?"

"I saw that strange man looking at you again last night."

Joan, was suddenly alert, in a flash she was sitting bolt upright in her bed. "Did you see what he looked like?" she asked, curious to find some form of identifying him.

"No, it was too dark and I only saw him from the back. But he reminded me of the man I saw outside the hospital when we arrived, he was the same build and had dark hair when he lifted his hat."

"Are you certain?" Joan, asked enthusiastically. "If it is him, then I think we ought to ask and find out who he is. And I would also like to know if any of the nurses who have slept in this room have seen him?" she added as she slid her feet into her slippers and raised herself from the bed. Just then, her mobile phone rang. "I`ll give you one guess who this is," she said, throwing a knowing look towards Anne, as she picked up the phone, and heard her husband`s voice.

Anne, didn't say anything, she just gave a shrug and disappeared into the bathroom.

"Hello love, just checking to see that you`re alright."

"We`re both fine," Joan, replied, "we are going into the basement after breakfast."

"Well, be careful," he warned, "remember what you told me about Harry, being too scared to go down there."

"Don`t worry love, we`ll be alright. I can take care of us both," she answered. trying to keep the tone light, even though her mind was fraught with worry after what Harry, had divulged to her.

"Well you take care. Call you later` love you," he said and without waiting for a reply he hung up.

`Bloody typical,` she grumbled. `He`s always in a rush.`

"I`ll bet that was dad," Anne, called from the bathroom as she brushed her teeth.

"You bet right! the same as usual he had to get to the yard to make sure all of the men and machines were up and running."

"Huh, that`s normal for him," Anne, gurgled through a mouthful of toothpaste.

Just then the phone rang again. Before she had the time to say hello, Joan, heard her husband telling her once again to be careful. "If you want me to come out there," he began.

"Oh for goodness` sake, Eric! I have told you that I am quite capable of looking after myself and Anne. And please do not ring while I`m working` I will call you when we have completed our investigation below.

"Be it on your own head I have offered," he retorted grumpily. Then before giving her the opportunity to reply, he rang off.

"Bloody men," she fumed, throwing her mobile down onto the bed.

When they were dressed and ready Joan, and Anne, made their way to the canteen, where they were surprised to find it almost empty. "That's odd," Anne remarked, when the four remaining nurses got up from their seats and left without saying a word, leaving them alone in the canteen. "I wonder what's wrong?" Anne, queried, looking at her mother.

"I've no idea," Joan, replied, equally as puzzled. "All I can assume, is that they must have heard about our planned visit to the basement today."

"Or that foul' mouthed Matron has told them to stay away from us' I believe that woman has something to hide," Anne, announced knowingly.

CHAPTER THIRTY EIGHT

THE KEYS

The silence and the vacant tables in the almost deserted canteen, created an uneasy atmosphere for Anne, and Joan. There was no hustle and bustle, nor chattering voices to be heard` even the women serving the hot breakfast who usually chatted to them, had withdrawn into the kitchen leaving them to serve themselves.

In an effort to break the silence, Anne, formulated conversation by speaking of trivialities until they had finished eating, before retreating to their room.

"I can`t understand what`s happening here. Why is everyone avoiding us?" Joan, remarked angrily, "they`re treating us like a pair of bloody lepers."

"Ignore it mother," Anne, remarked calmly. "We`ve got other things to think about, so forget about them."

Joan, acknowledged that Anne, was probably right in what she was saying and pulled on her heavy boots and thick clothing, then picked up the equipment they would be using. "Are you ready?"

"Ready when you are," Anne replied giving her a big smile.

"Right, we had better get moving then."

They picked up four thick candles and matches from the store room cupboard and two long handled brushes. Afterwards, they entered the canteen, where they stopped for a few moments to switch on the headlamps they were wearing, and took two of the candles from their pockets and lit them, before entering the dark, filthy corridor they had travelled through previously.

"I didn't think that spiders could weave their webs so quickly," Joan, commented as she brushed the diaphanous gossamer from her face, then held the candle high in front of her so the flame would immediately destroy the webs and revolting insects crawling through them. She did however feel a pang of conscience, when wondering if Anne, really wanted to be there.

"Are you certain you want to stay?" Joan, stopped to ask, "or would you rather go back to our room` after all, Harry, did say that it was very unpleasant what he saw down there. So I wouldn't hold it against you if you decided to go back?

"No way!" Anne, responded sharply` annoyed by her mother thinking that she would be so cowardly as to let her go on her own. "You don`t know what could waiting down there to pounce when you get into that basement. So you can forget about me going back` I`m not leaving you on our own mum! I`m coming with you."

"Alright, but stay close and don`t panic if anything happens," Joan, then forced herself to concentrate on getting through the maze of cobwebs, and didn't stop until coming to a door that was partially concealed beneath a mass of filth and webs. "This is the one we noticed the first time we came along here, isn't it?"

"Yes," Anne replied, "but we didn't stop to see where it led, did we? Instead you dragged me up that bloody awful staircase."

"Oh for goodness! sake! stop mithering," Joan snapped, as she pulled off her gloves and began trying to locate the key from the bunch that the Matron had given her. But In the darkness it was hard to differentiate one key from the other, as they all looked the same and there were so many on one loop to sort through. By now though, Joan`s, hands were cold and her fingers were practically numb` making it so uncomfortable for her that she could hardly hold the freezing metal keys .

"Damn!" she cursed, when she fumbled to place each key into the lock.

"Here let me have a go," Anne, said, moving her mother to one side and pulling off her gloves to take the keys from her mother's trembling fingers. "Your hands are freezing cold mum and so are the bloody keys," she cursed, "that's why you can't find the right one to fit the lock' you can't hold the dammed things properly!"

Joan, didn't argue and handed Anne the keys. Within minutes, Anne, had located the key to unlock the door and they were making their way down a flight of stone steps leading into the depths of the grim, desolate building, where it was colder still.

To their dismay however, they were stopped from proceeding any further, when finding a locked steel barred gate was blocking their way.

"Oh no! I don't have a key for this," Joan, let out a peeved moan, as she rummaged through the lloose key's in her pocket. "None of these will fit' they're are all too small," she groaned, pointing to the huge padlock. "Look at the size of that lock! the key to open that must be massive. Oh well, there's only one thing for it, I don't like doing this but"- She turned to face Anne. "You wait here, while I go back and get the key from Matron. If there are any obstacles on the way, I don't want you running into them."

"Oh no you won't," Anne, retorted bluntly. There was no way she was being left alone in the menacing darkness where she couldn't see if anything was creeping up behind her.

She didn't have to worry though, when they both unexpectedly heard Harry's voice, calling to them from above.

"Mrs Shepherd! Mrs Shepherd!" he called in a wavering tone. "Can you hear me? Please answer if you can' I don't want to come down there, it's too scary for me," his voice quivered as he spoke. "I have the key that will fit the gate, but you will have to come up for it, please Mrs Shepherd?"

"It's Harry," Anne, said, shining the light towards the top of the steps where she could just see the whiskery, old man, holding a large iron key in his hand. But from the look on his face in torch light, she could see that he was petrified and too scared to move any further forward than the top step.

"Go get the key from him will you?" Joan, expressed excitedly, "it`s crucial that we get into there as soon as possible` I want to see what he is so afraid of.

"I`m not sure that I want to either " Anne thought to herself.

"It`s alright Harry` I`m coming!" Anne, called, then hesitated for a moment and watched as her mother turned to concentrate on shining her lamp through the bars of the gate into the pitch, black murky area.

"For goodness, sake`" Anne, muttered to herself, then giving a sigh of resignation she turned and began carefully making her way up the stone steps that dipped in the centre, where they had worn away from abrasion after years of use. She had however, only moved up two of the steps when she sensed something moving very close beside her. "Oh no," she moaned, "what now." Within seconds she froze, not daring to move, her mind had stopped working clearly and had become a mixture of confused and befuddled thoughts.

"Mrs Shepherd! Mrs Shepherd!" she heard Harry, calling. "If you don`t come up here, then I will have to throw the key down to you and I`ll be gone."

"What on earth are you doing Anne? go get the key," she heard her mother calling impatiently.

The sound of her voice forced Anne, back to reality and she hurried forward, only to trip on the stone scraping her shins on the rough edge of the step, and cursed then called out to the caretaker. "What`s wrong Harry, why won`t you come down with the key ?" she shouted, shining her lamp into the darkness above, then stopped when seeing the uncharacteristic look on Harry`s face.

"I`m not coming down there," he called, and threw a large solitary key towards Anne, that bounced past her and clattered noisily down the steps, sending eerie reverberating echoes all around them in the daunting, oppressive darkness. "You`ll be needing more than that where you`re going," he shouted, then scurried away into the long dark passage.

"What the Dickins is wrong with him," Anne, muttered to herself and watched as the light from his lamp diminished from sight. Then after giving a sigh of resignation, she turned and made her way back down the precarious stone steps to pick up the heavy key and returned to her mother, who was still shining her torch into the chilly dark area and peering through the thick bars of the gate, in an attempt to see what lay beyond.

"Here mum` Harry, sent this," Anne, said, giving her mother a nudge. Startled by the unexpected touch, Joan, swung round and almost hit her daughter with the torch, but stopped when seeing who it was. "Bloody hell Anne, I almost hit you," she remarked, apologising profoundly.

"Mum calm down!" Anne, yelled, ducking to avoid the impending blow. "Harry gave me this," she expressed loudly, shining the light onto the key and holding it out to her mother.

"Oh love` I`m sorry, I almost-----.

"It`s alright mum, I understand` I should have said something before I touched you."

"Good grief it`s big," Joan, uttered, taking the enormous key into her hands, "and it`s heavy."

"You know what?" she scowled turning to face Anne. "I told, that bitch of a Matron this morning we were coming down here, so why the devil didn't she give me the key then?"

"Forget about her mum, we`ve got it now,"

"That`s not the point," Joan, griped, as she fumbled to unlock the gate. "By the way Anne," she added in a change of mood, "once were inside" she announced in a sombre tone, as the gate swung open, "whatever happens, do not show any sign of fear` or any presence in there, will latch onto it and take control over both your physical and mental abilities` do I make myself clear?"

"Bloody hell mum, you`re starting to sound like that f----- Matron."

CHAPTER THIRTY NINE

THE BASEMENT

Anne, felt a shiver of apprehension run through her, when together they stepped into the opaque stinking corridor. Directly they were through, they saw that it led along a straight, six feet wide passage. Joan, then closed the gate behind them. "I won`t lock it, in case we need to make a hasty retreat," she said as they shuffled cautiously forward, constantly aware that at any moment, something bizarre might appear alongside them.

Then, holding the long` handled brushes taken from the storeroom, and using their headlamps to guide them, Joan, and Anne, wielded the brushes from side to side and above their heads, to sweep away the aphid` riddled cobwebs dangling above their heads and encircling them. At times however they became affixed to their face and bodies as they struggled through the filthy passage. Also, the sickening sounds of their boots crunching upon small animal bones and vermin droppings, along with broken plaster that was strewn underfoot was demoralizing to say the least.

Eventually they managed to reach their destination and shone the brilliant light from both hand torches in front and above them. The light there revealed white, discoloured tiles covering the walls, that in the past had been covered with green paint and was now flaking from them. Adding to their bemusement, they were surprised to discover that when they came to the end of the passage, there was another door descending down two long wide steps, leading towards the basement onto another corridor. Once they were inside, they stopped and gazed about themselves in awe, when finding that the floor and walls were spotlessly clean. There was no sign of any vermin, cobwebs and dust, or the stench of mildew and decay that they had encountered on the upper floors` in fact, to their astonishment, the whole area they were now passing through, was immaculately clean.

"I don`t understand this," Joan, remarked, shining her light onto the walls and running her fingers over the ancient discoloured tiles. "By all accounts, I would have thought that this part of the building would have been dirtier than the first and second floors. Anne, you keep shining your light onto the walls and either side of this passage while I shine mine straight ahead` that way, we should have a good line of vision all around us. But stay close, I can`t see a bloody thing in this dark hole and I need to know where you are."

The passage was short, but confining and claustrophobic! whereby they were thankful when it opened out into a wider space. Then unpredictably, the moment they stepped in front of a dark, restrictive cubicle, the sounds of mournful cries and pitiful screams echoed all around them and a dim, red light appeared above the outside of the caged unit, lighting up the whole area. It revealed a rat infested, grimy, padded cell complete with dirty, fouled straw strewn across the floor, where a number of childlike, simpering figures of all ages were cowering against the walls. The poor, pathetic individuals were restricted from movement by straitjackets that fettered them by chains attached to the walls, rendering them helpless. However, immediately Joan, and Anne, stepped away from the cell, the light switched itself off and the sound stopped immediately.

"It`s a recording and the children are dummies, Joan, declared, stepping once again in front of the cell and flooding the area with the dull, red light and hearing the distressing cries again. "But why on earth? Should someone do this? ----" she spluttered. "Never mind that Mum, look at this?"

Anne, called, disrupting her mum`s furious thoughts. "look!" she said, pointing towards another cell.

The sight was appalling and shocked Joan, to the core` she couldn't take her eyes away from the distressing display when the light revealed the heart` rending sight. There was a group of emaciated young children crammed tightly together in one cell, who were huddled together with terrified expressions on their faces. Their naked bodies were covered with open, weeping sores and were shackled to the cold stone walls, with heavy chains and manacles. Adding to the sickening vision, was that the floor was infested with squeeling, robotic rodents feeding from the faeces caked straw, that was strewn across the floor of each cell.

"Oh dear God! How those poor souls must have suffered," Joan, groaned when, recognising the atrocities that had had been carried out in the name of medicine. "The gate must have been locked after the patients had been brought here, in order to prevent them from escaping when they began to understand in their confused minds, what sadistic treatment was going to be forced upon them," she stated furiously to Anne. .

CHAPTER FORTY

SHOCK IN THE MUSEUM

Despite the nauseating emotions they were feeling, both understood that the light and the pitiful cries had to be regulated by a well` coordinated, electrical system.

"*But why do this?*" Joan, wondered, "*could this have been in the old museum that they had heard so much about? But no! someone had said that it had been too gruesome to be on display and had been dismantled over twenty years ago. But if so, what was it doing down here intact in the basement?*"

Joan, tuned to her daughter. "Do you realise that we are in the abandoned psychiatric museum and operating theatre?"

"Of course I do," Anne, replied, stepping backwards and forwards in front of each of the six crowded cells, triggering the lights to turn on and off. "And have you wondered why the museum is being so well looked after? And why aren`t the artifacts and figures covered by dust sheets? Someone must be coming here on a regular basis to keep the mechanism in good working order."

"Oh! For goodness` sake Anne," she snapped angrily at her daughter. "Stop playing, and listen to what I am saying."

"I am listening," Anne carped, "I`m just giving us a bit of light while you`re looking round and working things out."

"Oh, right then, I think we should get moving and find out what is up-ahead."

Once again they found themselves in extreme darkness and freezing cold, when they passed the last of the holding cells, and then hesitated, when hearing muffled screams and wailing echoing eerily from the darkness directly ahead. "This sounds similar to the recordings we heard earlier," Joan, murmured, drawing to a halt and holding out her arm to prevent Anne, from proceeding any further.

"Where do you think it`s coming from?" Anne, whispered, shining her lamp in every direction, but couldn't see anything other than the discoloured, white tiled walls.

"I don`t know," Joan, murmured softly, "but I think it`s coming from behind that screen." "What screen?"

"That screen directly ahead of us, you idiot, can`t you see it." Joan, shone her lamp ahead of them, where they could see through the tattered, flimsy material of the screen was a door.

"Oh shit! not again," Anne whined, "I hope it isn't locked." They were dismayed however, after moving the screen to one side that there was a barred gate blocking their access to the door. Anne, leant forward and pulled at the gate, which to her astonishment it opened as soon as she drew back the bolt`, the door however was locked.

"Well, that's the first obstacle overcome," Joan, muttered and began rummaging through the loop of keys trying to find the right one to open the door, then stopped when hearing a man`s voice.

"Here, let me help."

Both women turned and found themselves face to face with a tall, dark` haired handsome man with brown penetrating eyes, offering to assist them. For a few moments they were too surprised to say anything, until Joan asked in a confused tone. "How did you get down here?"

"Simple, I work here," he replied, giving an engaging smile.

Joan, glanced towards Anne, who was staring at the stranger and noticed that he appeared to have the physique of a very powerful man.

"Its` alright, I`m a doctor, I help take care of the patients. "Warily Anne, shone her light across his clothing and saw that he was wearing a doctor`s white coat and had a stethoscope hung around his neck.

"We didn't hear you ------" her voice tailed off to a wheezing croak, when he suddenly faded away in front of them.

"Bloody hell mam!" was all Anne, managed to say, while Joan stood rooted to the spot in shock. "What do we do now?" Anne, quavered, totally stunned and at a loss after seeing and speaking to the apparition.

"I think he`s the same person we see at night in our room," Joan, declared, in a wavering tone.

"Mum?"

"What?"

"I`m scared."

"I`m feeling a bit that way myself," Joan, said without confidence, as she placed a pacifying hand on her daughters trembling arm.

"I don`t like it down here," Anne whimpered, "now we know why Harry was so afraid of coming here."

"Anne, we must concentrate on what we are doing` we can`t stop now that we have come this far." Joan`s voice was shaking, as she cast a cautious glance around them, that didn't go amiss from Anne`s ever observant eyes.

"You`re right mum," she replied, "but from now on, we have to be more vigilant. We don`t want any more unpleasant surprises creeping up on us when we go through that door."

CHAPTER FORTY ONE

THE MUSEUM ROBOTS

"For once in your life mum, will you be careful when we get in there? I know what you`re like."

"Don`t worry Anne," it will be alright," Joan, gave her a hug and a reassuring smile, then turned and rotated the huge cast iron handle and watched as the door swung slowly open.

"Follow me, but if I tell you to run, then run," Joan, commanded positively, as she stepped inside a large low ceilinged room followed by her tentative daughter.

The moment they stepped inside the room however, the door automatically closed and the whole area was flooded by a dim, red glow. Then to their horror they heard a loud click as the door locked, trapping them inside the room.

"Mum, what are we going to do?" Anne, screamed grabbing hold of Joan.

"Stay calm while I try to work something out," Joan shot back ferociously, as she swiftly scanned the encompassing area for another way out. She was then was struck dumb when observing the shocking spectacle, of macabre objects positioned around what appeared to be in an immaculately sterile area.

"What on earth," Joan, gasped.

"Mum," Anne, responded sharply, as she noticed the punishing equipment that in the past had been used on the incapacitated patients. "These are part of the museum pieces, look."

The shocking sight of models, representing patients who were being submerged in water by doctors and a male nurse in three deep metal baths, was almost too much for Joan to stomach. Each person had been secured by a leather thong being placed around their necks, that was passed through a metal loop attached to the bath. The patient had first been constrained, before being imprisoned in the bath. Then a thick wooden lid was placed across the top of the bath, to stop the poor, unfortunate creature from struggling to escape from the dreaded, ice` cold water.

Shaking her head in disbelief, Joan, walked over to read the notes of what was logged at the end of each tub, and saw that in their callous, scientific minds, the medical men had believed that with immersing the patients in freezing cold water, the shock would drive the insanity from the patient`s mind.

Meanwhile, Anne, was staring, appalled at two of the exhibits, where one of the three automated robots dressed in blood stained clothing, was operating on a patient that entailed the removal of part of the digestive and bowel organs. While on another table, a woman was having an abortion, followed by a sterilisation.

"Mum did they really do this to people? Anne, asked, hardly able to believe what she was seeing and reading.

"I`m afraid they did," Joan, replied. "It was all in the name of progress or so they assumed."

"Huh, somebody ought to have done it to them and then see if they believed it was in the name of progress."

Joan, turned away from the written documents and began to explain what one of the staff had informed her. "It was actually one of the Sisters who told me, that the patients who they were now caring for came from very wealthy families. They had paid to have their relations incarcerated in the asylum because they were an embarrassment to the families involved. Whereby, once they were placed in the asylum and a large amount of money had been paid for their upkeep, they were completely ignored by their relatives, and in layman`s words, forgotten. She also said that some of the funerals had been paid for in advance, but no one had attended them when the patient had died. Also she had never seen a burial service performed for any of the patients.

"Why?"

"I don`t know why," Joan snapped in frustration and began reading the notes at the bottom of each operating table, explaining why the operations were being carried out. "Just look here," Joan beckoned Anne to her side. "In the reports they state that insanity was caused by infection of the inner organs of the body, therefore the infected organs had to be removed. They also extracted most of the patient`s teeth, this was believed to help clean the whole of the patient`s system. Likewise when they removed the foetus from women, they alleged it was done with the best intensions, as the pregnancy was due to sexual intercourse between patients, therefore there was every chance that the woman would produce a child that would be born insane, so it had to be removed from its mother, who was then sterilized.

"She was most likely raped by one of the male nurses? Joan uttered angrily. "It did, and still does happen."

Then, there was also a lobotomy being carried out, Anne, was almost ill when she read and saw the procedure. This entailed an instrument akin to an ice pick being hammered through the patient`s skull below the eye lid, thus severing the connecting prefrontal cortex to the thalamus. On the following bed, was a man`s arched body in the throes of an electric shock treatment being carried out, five muscular men were holding the patient down` one held the head, others held the arms and legs. It was common knowledge that this treatment incurred dislocated limbs and left some patients permanently crippled.

Shocked and disgusted, Joan, and Anne, could barely comprehend the gruesome experimental events that had taken place in the name of medical advancement. The insane were regarded as non-human beings, therefore they were used for experimental purposes.

CHAPTER FOURTY TWO

THE MUSEUM GHOST`s

"Are you alright?" Joan, asked Anne, shining the light into a nearby area as they heard the sound of someone groaning, as if in acute pain, and was shocked into disbelief as they witnessed a macabre sight. In the dark confines of the cold, oppressive room was the reposing figure of a man, who appeared to be in agony, and was strapped into a stark, wooden reclining chair.

"Blinking heck mum! What`s that on his head.? Anne whispered.

"I don`t know," Joan replied peering into the dimly lit area. "It looks like some electronic contraption to me` maybe it was used for giving patients some sort of electric shock treatment." Joan answered, peering into where he was positioned, and shone the light directly onto the incapacitated figure.

Joan, who held steady on most occasions, felt her stomach lurch when seeing the gruesome spectre fastened onto the chair. It had a raw, bleeding wound near his eye, along with severe bruising across his face. And a mixture of mucus and blood ran down his chin into his long flowing beard. "Oh my God! " Joan croaked, Don`t look Anne, "these bloody dummies are too lifelike."

But her warning came too late! Anne, was rooted to the spot, staring in horror at the appalling sight of a man who was showing signs of malnutrition. His skin was pulled so taut against his skull that it looked as if would tear at any given moment. By all appearances the man had never been washed` there were chucks of hair missing from his head, and his body oozed with weeping, septic sores. The thin straggly remaining hair on his head was a long entangled mess that fell to his waist. His upper torso was bare revealing every bone of his ribcage, and the lower part of his body was covered by a dirty piece of old linen.

For a few heartrending seconds, the man stared helplessly towards Joan, then began making strange guttural sounds as he fought against his restraints. Adding to the shock of the nauseating sight, he abruptly vanished and within seconds the whole scenario reverted back to the robotic replicas of human beings.

"Mum! Mum! Anne screamed, grabbing hold of Joan and clinging to her. "I thought he was a dummy, but he wasn`t! Was he. He was a ghost! Mum, what are we going to do?" Anne, croaked.

Joan, however, couldn't answer at that moment she was rendered speechless.

"I thought it was a dummy?" Anne, muttered keeping hold of her mum` she too afraid to let go in case something else happened.

"You`re not the only one." Joan, replied in a shaky voice, hugging her daughter close. "I`m just as scared as you are."

"Mum?"

"What?"

"There has to be a generator down here to make these figures move and to switch on the subdued lighting."

"That`s what I was thinking," Joan replied, "and I intend to find out exactly where it is."

CHAPTER FORTY THREE

THE GENERATOR

Joan, and Anne, avoided looking at the rest of the gruesome exhibits as they made their way out of the museum and through a low arched doorway, to begin searching for the generator.

"The generator has to be close to the mechanical presentations," Joan, said, shining her lamp and lighting up the small chamber they had entered, "or the exhibits and lights wouldn't be able to work so quickly Even so it would make the job easier if we had some power in here." She called to her daughter. "Can you find a light switch anywhere on the wall?"

"No I can`t," Anne, replied shining the torch over the walls, then felt a flicker of anxiety pass through her, when her torch began to splutter on and off." "Oh no, please don`t go out not now! Please don`t let the battery go flat!" she uttered softly, hoping that her mother wouldn`t notice the diminishing beam, and began shaking her torch until the light came back on again.

"I think it is over here," Joan, called, "I can hear something whirring behind this pile of disused equipment accumulated here. So be careful where you put you`re, feet and try not to bump into anything."

"*Easier said than done,*" Anne thought to herself, as she began working her way past the dismantled medical equipment, then felt her stomach churn when catching sight of the old mortuary tables and dissecting apparatus, and balked when seeing the faded anatomy and dismembering charts still hanging on the wall.

Nevertheless, despite the repugnant findings, Anne`s curiosity got the better of her and she stopped to read the charts which had been hung there for teaching purposes, these described dismembering methods for students in the medical profession, when using the unwanted cadavers for dissecting and experimental studies after the patient`s, death. There was also a declaration, stating that after the medical students had finished cutting open the corpses, then the remains were to be disposed of in any way fit.

"Blood hell!" she gasped. "Mum come take a look at this!"

"What have you found now?" Joan asked coming to her side.

Anne, shone the light onto the faded charts and notices, showing the graphic illustrations and literature describing the experimental studies carried out on the unfortunate, defenceless people who were held there against their will.

Not all of the individuals however, had been insane. Joan discovered when reading, that the hospital had at one time been a workhouse for the poor, these people had gone to work there in exchange for food and medical treatment that only the wealthy could afford. Along with the poor and destitute, were young women and girls who had been servants at country houses` they had become impregnated by male members of the wealthy families. Because of their pregnancy, they had been declared insane and were sent to the workhouse as they had no means of support. Their families could not afford extra mouths to feed, and had turned their backs on them leaving the poor girls to their own devices. In order to survive some of the wretched girls had died from botched unhygienic abortions, while others turned to prostitution to survive. But sadly they had later succumbed to sexually transmitted diseases.

In time, one part of the workhouse had become a hospital for the poor people in the vicinity, where unwanted babies and young children were supposedly put up for adoption, and the other part of the hospital, became an asylum for the criminally insane.

"I can`t believe it," Joan, exclaimed furiously, "I`m going to take all of this information with me when we leave."

"But mum."

"What?"

Before Anne, could add anything further, she felt a hand gently touching her shoulder and froze. At the corresponding time, Joan, felt herself undergoing a similar bizarre sensation, when sensing that someone was attempting to communicate with them. "Who are you she asked? What do you want?"

At first there was an unmitigated silence and nothing happened, until they heard a young woman`s voice asking where her baby was. "Find my baby, where is she?" the voice pleaded.

"I don`t know," Joan replied, but perhaps I could find out, if I knew who you are?"

"I`m Millie, I`m fourteen years old, and I worked at the Verity mansion before I was sent here by the mistress." The girl began to wail before breaking down into sobs of pitiful tears. Please, please find my baby" the voice wailed as it petered, then faded away.

Joan was almost overcome by emotion and turned towards her daughter then gasped in alarm when noticing the peculiar, impassive look on her face. "Anne, pull yourself together," she shouted, reaching out and shaking her hoping to get a reaction. Then stopped and drew back when seeing in the wide beam of her head lamp, an assembly of phantom soldiers and airman grouped together, standing beside her daughter. "Oh my God," she whispered softly. "Anne! Anne! You must remain calm! Just stay where, you are and do not move."

But before she could say any more, Anne, despite being overcome by uncertainty and the lack of confidence, used every effort to retain her composure and stated calmly. "It`s alright mum, I know they are here."

CHAPTER FORTY FOUR

THE PHANTOM SERVICEMEN

Joan`s brain was spinning, as she fought to make the decision of what step to take next the most important objective however, was the safety of her daughter. Nevertheless, she had no need to worry, when Anne, unexpectedly, enquired as to the apparition`s whereabouts.

"Are they still behind me?" she asked in a wobbly voice.

"No, they have moved over towards one of the mortuary tables," Joan, replied.

"Something bad must have happened to them in here then," Anne, said, as she turned her gaze over to the dissecting tables, then felt her legs go weak when seeing the ethereal transparent figures of four, bedraggled soldiers in WW2 uniforms and two RAF pilots. "Oh my God!" she gasped at the awesome sight, then quickly pulled herself together when absorbing the distressed and sorrowful looks on their faces. "Oh mum! Can`t we do something to help them, they look so sad, she wailed, turning to Joan. "I wonder if their families know where they died? I`m certain that it must have been here." At precisely the moment Anne, spoke, every item in the room began to vibrate, then quickly became calm again.

"It`s all right mum," she cried excitedly, "they must have been here at some time or the other or they wouldn't have responded as they did."

As if one of the airmen understood what she was saying, he raised his arm and pointed towards another door that had gone unnoticed by the women prompting, it to swing open unaided, and saw that it led into a dark, abandoned, circular chamber. "I`m game if you are?" Anne, said confidently, heading towards the gaping, black, open doorway.

Joan nodded, but within seconds of them entering the small enclosure, the whole area was suddenly engulfed in a brilliant white light, and they found that the group of servicemen were already in there waiting for them, standing beside an old, disused well. The stone well standing in the centre of the chamber was roughly three feet high. Sealing its top was a large, circular, wooden structure with a huge, cast iron loop in its centre. Built on either side of the well was a solid wooden frame and fitted to the overhead beam was a hoist, this had a large, metal hook inserted into the chain at the end of the hoisting mechanism that was wrapped around the top rafter of the thick, solid joist of timber.

"Now we know where they are," Joan remarked grimly, shaking her head. "We must not touch anything and we have to inform the police about this right away," Within seconds the group of servicemen had disappeared. "What? Where? How?" Joan ranted anxiously, as she spun around staring into every corner of the room, "where have they gone?"

"Never mind where have they gone. I have to go back I`ve hurt myself and torn my pants."

"Anne, wait just a moment` look over by the wall, the generator, I knew it was close, it`s beside the wall` that's why we could hear it, it is opposite the wall where I was-----."

"Forget about the bloody generator mum!" Anne shouted above the noise her mother was making, as she pushed objects away from the generator. "I`m bleeding."

Joan stopped what she was doing and turned towards her daughter. "Eh? what are you talking about?"

"I said I have hurt myself and torn my jeans on something sharp."

"You`ve what?"

"I bumped into something earlier and I cut my leg` I need to get back to our room and take a look at it," Anne, snapped, frustrated by her mother`s insistence at finding the generator.

Joan, moved over to Anne, and glanced down at her torn pants where she saw the tear and the blood stain that was slowly spreading across the thick cloth of her jeans. "Oh my goodness! why didn't you say something sooner?" her mum whispered, shocked by the appalling sight.

"Because you were too busy with your bloody ghosts," Anne retaliated angrily.

"Come on, I`d better get you upstairs and get one of the nurses to take a look at that," Joan, began hustling her daughter towards the door.

"That`s the most sensible thing you`ve said today," Anne, snapped angrily, as they hurried past the gruesome operating rooms and padded cells and didn`t stop until reaching the iron gate, which they swiftly passed through, and only hesitated long enough to lock it securely before moving quickly up the stairs into the long, gloomy corridor.

For a few moments, the pair felt a sense of relief at being out of the basement and thought their troubles were over, until they noticed something encased in an eerie, fluorescent glow moving towards them.

"Mum," Anne, groaned, "I can`t take any more."

Neither can I Joan, thought, holding her daughter close. "It`s alright, it can`t hurt you` I won`t let it," she said with conviction.

As the radiating figure drew closer, they observed a young woman in a nurse`s uniform, who appeared totally unaware of their presence, they watched as the bizarre figure drew closer. Then to their surprise the apparition floated straight by and disappeared into the opaque, gloomy confines of the corridor.

"Mum, I`m frightened," Anne whispered. "I know, so am I," Joan, replied, hugging her trembling daughter even closer, "but it`s going to be alright love` only we have to get moving, I`ve got to get you out of here, and get you some help with your injured leg."

CHAPTER FORTY FIVE

SAFE RETURN

"What`s happened to you two? You look as if you`ve seen a ghost!" the matron sniggered, when they staggered into the canteen with Joan supporting Anne, who helped her to a seat and propped her injured leg onto another chair.

Joan had no time to argue with the Matron, nor was she in any mood to listen to her offensive remarks. At that moment, her top priority was to get medical assistance for her daughter and she was quickly running out of patience after their latest bizarre encounter to tolerate any more insufferable behaviour from the belligerent female.

Infuriated, Joan, turned towards her and gave her a word of warning in front of the entire staff who were seated watching the scenario taking place in the canteen. "I had better warn you before you say anymore," Joan cautioned her in an exasperated tone, "that all conversation that takes place while I am investigating this hospital, is being recorded, and it will be reported back to the Trustees. Do I make myself clear? You Matron are supposed to be helping, not hindering. Now get out of my way and tell one of the staff to attend to my daughter`s injured leg immediately!"

The Matron couldn't believe what she was hearing` an outsider talking down to her and telling her what to do! Infuriated, she turned to the nurse sitting the closest to them. "Sort this woman out," she snapped, then strutted away, knowing that Joan, had thrown down the gauntlet and she had just lost the challenge.

CHAPTER FORTY SIX

PHENOMENA IN THE WARD

Anne showered, then sat patiently waiting, as Nurse Morris cleaned and dressed the wound on her leg in the treatment room, while Joan contacted the police to inform them of her suspicions.

"It isn't serious, but you will have to change the dressing daily," Nurse Morris told Anne, "and I will arrange for you to have a tetanus jab to avoid any infection. We don't know how long that equipment has been down there or if it was rusty. You must have the injection as a precaution," she asserted positively.

"I hate injections," Anne groaned. Before she could complain any further, Joan, arrived to informed Anne, that she would be returning to the basement with the police, to lead them down to the chamber where the well was situated. And to indicate because of the strange smell to where she suspected the remains of the unclaimed patients' had been discarded.

"I'm coming with you." Anne declared rising unsteadily to her feet. "No you're not' you have had a nasty shock and hurt yourself, so you are staying here," Joan, told her.

"But I want to be there when they are ------."

"I said no. You are staying here," Joan responded sharply. Joan then dropped a bombshell.

"I think I ought to ring your father to come and take you home."

"No," Anne, yelled leaping to her feet. "I can`t leave you here on your own mum` especially with that bloody old dragon Elliot!"

Just then, a piercing shriek rang out from the first ward, sending Joan, Anne, and Nurse Morris, racing to the ward, where they were just in time to witness an emaciated figure of a young woman, draped in dirty, ragged clothing` rise from a chair, then float over to the wall and dissolve through it.

"Oh my God," the Nurse moaned, who had been attending to a patient as she promptly fell to the floor in a dead faint`, while the patient in contrast was sitting cackling with laughter, pointing to the wall that the apparition had passed through.

"Quick, help me get her onto the chair!" Joan, shouted to Anne, above the din the patient was making. Together they lifted the stricken nurse to her feet and sat her down in the chair where, the apparition had been seated.

"It`s alright," Joan, spoke in a comforting tone, as she slowly began to recover. "Whatever was here, has gone."

"But it was sat in this chair," the nurse shrieked hysterically, trying to get to her feet, but Joan, pushed her back down again. "It wasn't real, it was just an apparition you saw. It is nothing to be afraid of, perhaps you will feel better if you go and lay down for a while?"

"But I can`t leave the patients," she moaned and began weeping .

"Anne" Joan, called to her daughter. "Will you go tell the Matron what has happened?"

"Oh glory! not me!"

"I said" Joan, was beginning to lose her patience, "that I told you to go and get the Matron now.

"Oh for goodness sake, I heard you! I get all the rotten jobs," Anne, grumbled as she left the ward to find the Matron.

CHAPTER FORTY SEVEN

WHERE ARE THEY

Nurse, Margaret Johnson, a stocky five and a half feet tall, woman, began telling Joan, of the odd and weird happenings that were occurring in the other three occupied wards and the recreation room. The scary phenomenon had started, she informed Joan, and glanced furtively around the ward to ensure that no one would over hear what she had to say. Was while they were in the recreation room entertaining the patients. A large number of table tennis balls had appeared from out of nowhere and had begun pelting the staff and patients about their heads and bodies. The patients had thought it was hilarious and part of the games, and had howled with laughter at the unprecedented fun. The staff however, who were taken by surprise by the unexpected phenomena, had tried to dodge and avoid being hit by the balls, until the mysterious phenomena stopped as suddenly as it began, and the balls evaporated into thin air.

On another occasion, the staff had watched helplessly in the wards, while chairs and beds with patients in them, had been lifted and floated to different parts of the ward. But when the nurses had tried to run and get help, a number of the beds had slid up to the doors, barring their exit. Upon hearing the nurses petrified screams and the moronic laughter coming from the patients in ward two, the Matron had rushed into the ward to see what was causing the noisy, raucous disturbance. Inevitably, she found that everything was in chaos, nonetheless the moment the patients caught sight of the Matron, they immediately slid under the bedcovers giggling and shrieking with uncontrollable laughter. Yet, in unquestionable fear of her uncontainable temper. "What is going on here?" she demanded to know. "Nurse return these beds back into the position where they belong. "Before she could utter another word, one of the nurses told her to do it herself` she was leaving` and walked out of the ward.

"What?" the red faced Matron had stuttered, staring after her in disbelief. She was unaccustomed to anyone turning their back on her. She was however further undermined when hearing jeers and chuckles emanating from beneath the bedcovers. Fuming, the Matron marched over to the first bed, from where most of the noise was coming from and pulled back the bedcovers` then reeled back in shock, when finding no one there! Infuriated and filled with disbelief, she marched over to each bed and drew back the covers, but every bed was the same` there were no patients in them. "Where the hell are they?" she shouted at the frightened nurses. No one dare move or speak. "I asked` where are they?"

She turned her furious gaze onto Joan, and Anne. "You must know something!" she shrieked losing all of her professional conduct. "You all heard them? I repeat` where are they?" she yelled pointing to the empty beds, "they can`t have just disappeared into nowhere`." Before anyone could reply, the staff gaped in astonishment, when seeing the patients being returned one by one` to their beds, looking just as stunned as the rest of them. "Oh my God" the Matron gasped, as her face drained of colour, staring about the ward in helpless frustration. "Where were they? Where have they been?" she shrieked in exasperation. Then with a loud thud she slumped to the floor unconscious.

"Oh no,! Nurse Johnson cried, staring down at the Matron. "Somebody help me to lift her."

"Well I`m not touching her` she`ll go mad if she finds out if I`ve laid a finger on her," the security guard expressed optimistically, who had been alerted by the racket and stared down at the Matron`s bulky form laying on the floor.

"Well I can`t lift her and neither can Anne," Joan remarked in no uncertain terms, "so she will have to stay there until she can get up on her own."

As Joan and the guard were discussing what to do, Anne took one of the pillows from a patient`s bed and placed it beneath the Matron`s head, in an effort to make her comfortable, while the patients sat giggling on their beds, pointing to the Matron who was lying motionless on the floor. Joan, however, had assessed the situation and gone over to the Sister`s desk to pick up the ward telephone to call for assistance and relate what had happened. Whereupon the receptionist had immediately sent two, burly male nurses to lift the Matron, but by the time they arrived the Matron had regained consciousness and was sitting up on the floor, claiming that she was alright and didn't need any help.

CHAPTER FORTY EIGHT

POLICE.

Joan's head was swimming after being asked the same questions over and over again by the police: `What were the patients doing at the time of the Matron's collapse? Were any of the patients responsible? Were they all in their beds when the incident occurred? Did any one of them push her to the floor? Did one of the nurses push her?` and so on, until Joan, felt as if her head was about to explode.

Later when Joan, and Anne, were sat alone in their room holding a freshly brewed mug of coffee in their hands, Joan's voice was flat and hardly audible when she spoke. "I can hardly believe what is happening, we only came to investigate the reported phenomena for the Trustees, but I never expected this." She sighed in exasperation.

"Neither can I," Anne, replied, "I've rung dad and told him what has happened, and he thinks we should leave immediately, before something equally unpleasant happens to us."

"But we can't leave, the police have said that no one has to vacate the building."

"But mum." Anne, said, placing a comforting arm around her mother's shoulders, "there is no longer a reason for us to stay, you did explain to them why we were here, so what is the problem?"

"The problem is, there could be a number of dead bodies in that well in the basement, that's what the problem is," Joan proclaimed wearily. Almost two hours had passed since the police had spoken to them, before the officer in charge of the investigation, Sergeant John Andrews, had arrived to ask Joan, if she would accompany him and his men down to the basement to show him where the chamber could be located. "Of course," Joan, had replied. "But you are going to need strong lights down there, as it is pitch black, due to the power being switched off in that part of the hospital."

"Hum, that shouldn't be too much of a problem," he declared thoughtfully` rubbing his chin. Joan didn't wait for him to say anything further before stating, "I did find a small scale generator in the chamber though, but I think it only provides power for the museum exhibits."

"What exhibits?" he asked in surprise.

"You will see when you get there," she said unenthusiastically and left it at that.

The Sergeant had decided that from the look of Joan, and her daughter, they had suffered enough trauma and for the time being he didn't push the subject any further. Instead he ordered his men to arrange for arc lights to be sited along the dark, dingy corridor and also positioned in the chamber containing the well.

Then when everyone was ready, Joan, proceeded to lead them to their appointed destination. Sergeant Andrew`s and his men however, weren't prepared for carting the heavy electrical equipment along the filthy, twisting corridors until reaching the locked gate leading into the museum.

But when they had finally reached the locked gate, Joan, stopped and told them, that what they were about to encounter was not what they would be expecting, and to prepare themselves for the sight of the unexpected atrocities that had been carried out there in the past. Some of the officers who were totally unaware of what was in that area nudged one another and sniggered, but soon pulled themselves together once they had stepped through into the museum and seen the working exhibits.

At first all that could be heard were gasps of shock and curses, until the men had calmed down after witnessing the devastating sight, when they trod on the switch`s controlling the dim, red light that illuminated each tiny cell.

"Come on lads, we`ve got a job to do. Stop mucking about and let`s get moving." The Sergeant barked. immediately the six officers stood to attention.

"We have to pass through that door over there to get to the room where the small generator is situated, before we reach the well," Joan informed him. "But from then on, be careful," she advised him.

"Right," he nodded, then directed his men into the next squalid room, where he stood waiting impatiently until all of the equipment had been brought through. "Is that the door?" he asked Joan, indicating towards the one that had been previously locked as soon as Joan, and Anne, had passed through, she then and warned the Sergeant of what would happen once they were all in the room. "If you could get out, then we can," he added gruffly. "Okay lads," he shouted to the officers, "once we`re inside, I want you Barnes, to be ready to shove something heavy between the frame and that door to stop it from shutting. "Alright lads, let`s get started."

On the Sergeants command the men pushed open the door, Barnes placed a heavy electric arc light on the top step barring the door from closing, and stayed alongside it to ensure that it stayed open, while the rest of the men assembled inside the room.

However, as soon as he entered the chamber, Sergeant Andrews immediately recognised the odour of decayed human flesh and turned towards Joan, requesting that she should leave before they opened up the well.

"Before I go, would you allow me to say a prayer for whoever may be down there?" she asked indicating towards the well.

"Of course," he replied removing his cap and signalled for his men to do likewise, and they lowered their heads in respect, as Joan began to pray for the lost souls entombed in the bleak depressive confines of their final resting place.

CHAPTER FORTY NINE

THE WELL

After Joan, had reluctantly left the officers to carry out their work, Sergeant Andrews informed his men to prepare themselves for what they would find down there and ordered Officers Johnson, and Rawlings, to remove the lid covering the stone structure.

Affixed to the wooden joist at the side of the well, was a large wheel set in a metal frame! this was connected to a thick, heavy duty chain that ran from the wheel and up the side of the joist to the chain containing the hook above. Officer Johnson had lowered the metal hook down to the hefty wooden lid, while Rawlings fitted the hook over the handle of the lid, then started winding the wheel handle to raise the cover.

But within minutes of him turning the wheel alongside the apparatus, everyone who had been clustered around the perimeter waiting to see what was inside the well, gasped and fell back choking, when the revolting stench of dead and decaying flesh swept across the entire chamber.

"Close it! Close it!" the Sergeant yelled loudly, "leave the fucking lights and get the hell out of here." Gasping and choking the Sergeant and his team raced from the gruesome chamber, and once they were through the filthy passage and inside the canteen, to where Joan, and Anne, were waiting. Immediately they were all safely inside the canteen, Joan got to her feet and hastily locked the door, while Sergeant Andrews rang through to the forensic team telling them to drop everything they were doing and get to the asylum as quickly as possible. And to bring heavy lifting gear, extra men, breathing apparatus and an abundance of body bags.

CHAPTER FIFTY

GOING TO THE ATTIC

Sergeant Andrews gave Joan, permission for her and Anne, to examine the attic on the top floor of the asylum, as it was the only place in the building that she and Anne had not yet investigated. He did however, insist that they should not go anywhere near the basement, but he kindly offered the services of one of his officers, Constable Jim Bates to accompany them, if by chance they should run into any problems and might need help.

Joan, was satisfied by the Sergeant's terms, she was only too pleased at the thought of having the officer going along with them to guarantee their safety and wellbeing. She was however, concerned about her daughter, as she had reacted badly on the last occasion when she had panicked and injured herself. Nevertheless, Anne, had told her mother that she wanted to accompany her to the attic. Not only that, but she wasn't going to leave her alone with a total stranger who knew nothing about psychic phenomena.

They were surprised by the appearance of Constable Bates when he arrived, he wasn't at all what they expected. He stood over six feet tall, and Joan guessed that he was about thirty years of age, his face had a rugged, well-worn look about it, that was surrounded by a mop of dark brown hair, his shoulders were wide and he was built like an ox. It was obvious that at first sight, he was a no-nonsense man who could be relied upon if any problems should arise, his whole demeanour made Joan feel more secure by his very presence.

The only problem was, that he scoffed at the idea of ghosts, saying they were all old wives` tales that were told to frighten naughty children, and to scare people away from certain places. Also, they were more likely to be figments of a person`s overactive imagination` Joan, and Anne, knew better. They did however, warn him not to scoff at what he didn't understand and explained to him the possibilities of what could happen, especially when they were alone in the bleak, haunted passages of the asylum.

But he still scoffed at the idea of ghosts.

Even when Joan, explained to Bates, that they were going into an area of the building that was reputed to be haunted and they hadn`t yet investigated, he just laughed. "Not only that," she informed him, "But the basement where the Sergeant and the forensic team are now working was an extremely haunted area. They could hardly believe it when he scoffed, saying that he had heard it all before, and as far as he was concerned, all the tales of ghost`s and hauntings, were concocted to frighten vagrants and junkies away from the empty asylum.

Bates did however, begin having second thoughts when he observed gleaming orbs of light dart through the beam of his torch, that disappeared immediately they were noticed. Feeling slightly unnerved, Bates gripped the cast iron bar tightly, that he had brought along to protect himself and the two women if it was deemed necessary.

But as they slowly made their way up the main staircase, across the first balcony then up more stairs to the second balcony and were about to move towards the staircase leading up into the attic, Bates drew to an abrupt halt when a distorted, glowing shape darted past him and disappeared into the dark recess of the corridor.

"Bloody Hell!" he uttered, then let out a yell of alarm, when a mass of hanging cobwebs complete with enormous aphids unexpectedly draped themselves across his face and clothing, while instantaneously his boots crunched over the dried up bones of long dead creatures that had perished there over the years.

"Shit, shit, shit!" he yelled, as he attempted to dash the obnoxious vermin away from himself as they scampered over his hands and uniform. At the same time, he found it hard to ignore the strange sounds emanating from the empty wards opposite. He then almost leapt out of his skin, as he unexpectedly heard the voice of Jack, the caretaker, as he came towards them shining his torch in their direction.

"Blood hell man" you nearly scared the shit out of me`" Bates quivered hoarsely, then apologised to the women for his bad language.

"It`s alright, were used to it," Anne, gave a sarcastic laugh as she spoke. "You should try living with my dad, then you would know what bad language is."

"You`re right there," Joan, added, agreeing with Anne.

"Where are you going?" Jack, asked, interrupting their sarcastic comments. "I hope it isn't up there." He motioned towards the attic with his torch. Anyway Matron would never give you the key`s for the attic," he added in a know all manner. "She always keeps them to herself, an Ide like to bet the old bugger sleeps with them under her pillow," he said giving a low grating chuckle.

"That`s where you`re wrong," Joan, said, removing the key`s from her pocket and sticking them in Jack`s face. "After a few significant words, I managed to get the keys from her.

"Keys? How many keys do you need to get into one room?" he asked, puzzled by this new piece of information.

"Never mind how many! We are about to go into the attic, you can come if you want to?" she offered, holding out her hand to him.

"You have to be joking," he mumbled, "you won`t get me up there. "He then turned and disappeared into the darkness, grumbling to himself about the dangers of the entire malevolent building.

CHAPTER FIFTY ONE

PHENOMENA ON THE STAIRCASE

The first key unlocked the steel barred gate, that at first was stiff and hard to move, but with the help of Officer Bates, he managed to pull it open wide enough to allow all three of them to pass through into the modest` sized alcove at the bottom of the staircase.

Joan then sorted through the next three keys before finding the correct one to unlock the door in front of them. But before she had the chance to use it, to their surprise the door opened of its own accord, compelling a weird formidable sensation to spread through them.

"Holy shit," Bates exclaimed, jumping back in alarm. "What the hell`s happening?"

"Don't worry about it," Joan told him, "stay calm, nothing is going to harm you! it`s only the spirit`s way of letting you know that they are with us and are trying to help."

"Alright, if you say so, but I think we should return to-----"

"No way," Anne snapped, "we are here to carry out an investigation and that is precisely what we are going to do. If you want to go back then go."

Bates was taken aback by Anne`s, unwavering attitude, therefore as he had a reputation to keep as being a hard, tough man, he pulled himself together and decided to go along with the two women rather than appear to be afraid of ghosts.

"Before we go any further," he added, "would you please call me Bates? Officer Bates, and Miss, and Mrs Shepherd, seems to be a bit too formal considering the situation we are dealing with."

"That's alright by me," Joan, added with a smile, "I'm Joan, and this is my daughter, Anne. Now that we have got the introductions out of the way, shall we continue?"

Bates, still couldn't help but feel a sense of anxiety, as he proceeded ahead of them and shone his torch up the staircase into the dark, uninviting region above, where the beam revealed a set of twelve steep steps leading up towards a chained, padlocked door. "Oh no, I can't believe this," Joan, groaned irritably. "Now I've seen it all."

In single file they guardedly began climbing the narrow stairs and stopped when reaching the padlocked door, where Joan, reached up and switched on her headlamp, then clipped her torch to the belt around her waist, so that she would have her hands would be free to undo the padlock. "Shine your torch on my hands Anne, I need the extra light, so I can see what I'm doing," she requested as she rummaged in the grim shadows to find the right key to fit the padlock.

However, the moment Joan asked for extra light, the chain inexplicably fell away and the padlock opened and dropped onto the top stair. In turn, both the chain and padlock subsequently rattled all the way down the staircase and disappeared into the darkness to the floor below. "Oh bloody hell." Jim, shouted jumping away in fright when the gate swung open automatically. Even Joan, and Anne, took a step back in surprise and gawked in awe at the unexpected happening.

"What do we do now?" Bates, asked shakily, "I think we should,------"

"No" Anne, interrupted, as he was making a move to leave, and grabbed hold of his coat sleeve to stop him.

"But it's not safe!" he blustered.

"Safe or not, we are staying' we have to find out what is in the room behind that door."

"Look, I came here to accompany you two up to the attic, which I've done, and not go searching for bloody spooks."

Furiously, he pulled his arm away from Anne's grasp then began making his way down the gloomy staircase. Then stopped with the realisation that he would be unaccompanied when he would have to go through the intimidating darkness and pass the unapproachable, menacing rooms on both floors of the asylum before reaching the staircase to escape the terrifying area. Bates, however, was also afraid that he would come up against the ghostly manifestation of someone who had died there. With that thought in mind, he decided that he should stay and reluctantly climbed the stairs to re-join the women.

In the meantime Joan, had managed to regain her composure and had warily stepped forward to check the door mechanism to ensure that it was locked. But to her surprise the door unpredictably swung open, to expose an intensely dark and damp atmosphere from where the nauseating odour, of strong chemicals infiltrated their nostrils.

CHAPTER FIFTY TWO

ATTIC INVESTIGATION

"Oh good grief! what have they been doing up here?" Joan, gasped, covering her nose against the offensive stench.

"I don`t know, but think I should go first," Bates, expressed firmly, edging Joan, to one side. "We don`t know who or what could be restrained in there." The officer then grasped the crowbar in his hand, ready for any sign of trouble as he sidled past Joan, then gently eased the door further open, shining the light directly ahead of himself. He knew that if anyone had been stood waiting to pounce near the doorway, then the light from his powerful torch would have blinded them. Nevertheless, he couldn't help but feel a sense of uncertainty as he stepped into the weird, inhospitable freezing cold area.

In the meantime Joan, and Anne, were huddled together listening for any unusual sounds and shone their lights behind them to ensure no one was watching, while they waited for Bates, to signal that it was safe for them to enter the room.

Meanwhile, they could hear him stumbling about in the extreme darkness as he checked the whole space for anything that could be detrimental to them, and after a short while he appeared at the door telling them that it was safe for them to enter. "It`s not very big," he declared, flashing his lamp about the area, "but it looks to me as if somebody has wanted to seal this part of the attic off from the rest of the roof space." He began thumping with his huge fist on the walls that appeared solid, but when he thudded on the opposite wall, the sound reverberated back. "This is a partition` somebody has wanted a smaller room," he declared thoughtfully, as he swept his hands across the entire wall. "But for what reason?" he puzzled, then turned to warn Anne, as he saw her going towards the wall opposite to find out what was placed there. "Be careful," he warned, I banged my head on those beams over in the far corner," he cautioned, "so take care that roof is a bit low over there." Anne acknowledged what he was saying, nevertheless she was grateful of his presence as it gave her strong sense of security. However, due to his hight Bates, was having to stoop as he attempted to survey almost everything in the confined ten feet square attic space.

At the first glance, they could see the that the room was moderately clean and there was no sign of vermin, plus there was only a slight coating of dust that had settled on top of the five cupboards beneath two levels of shelves that lined two of the walls. However, placed on the cupboards were two heavy brass candlestick holders, these held three candles each which appeared to have been used recently, due to the melted candle wax that had run down the stems affixing them to the cupboard tops.

In the centre of the room stood a strong, metal` framed table with a raised edge containing a drainage system, alongside of this was a small, two tier trolley draped with a sheet of white linen. When Anne, lifted it, she saw that it held a number of sharp surgical instruments.

Positioned beneath the table were four white, chipped, enamelled buckets containing rubber tubes, cloths and various objects, together with a single upright chair situated at the lower end of the table. And on the floor to their right, was a number of large and various sized empty glass jars, and a large wooden cask standing on a low metal frame with a tap at the lower edge. This left them wondering, what was the room used for?

"There`s a door in this wall over here," Bates, called, shining his torch onto a metal` studded, wooden door, "it`s different from the others," he declared, with a thunderous boom of excitement.

"I wonder if should we take a look and see what`s in there?"

"I don`t know, what do you think mum?" Anne, asked Joan, who was busy examining the contents of the jars, and moved to his side.

"Well we won`t know until we look, will we?," she replied, "but you had better be careful" she added, hiding the cheeky grin on her face, knowing that Bates was now becoming a nervous wreck and afraid of his own shadow.

Anne, held up her arms and began acting the fool by waving her hands about, imitating a ghoulish figure and creating bloodcurdling noises. "Something might be waiting to grab you." She moaned and burst out laughing when seeing the startled look on his face.

CHAPTER FIFTY THREE

WHAT IS IN THE JARS

Taking hold of the cast iron handle, Bates, pushed at the door, but the door was stuck and appeared not to have been opened for many years! and it barely moved a few inches on its rusted, creaking hinges before stopping.

"Keep back, and be ready to get out fast," he warned, as he braced himself to force the door open, "and be ready to run."

"What do you think is in there?" Anne, whispered anxiously to Joan, as they shuffled over to the open door at the top of the staircase, all of the time watching nervously as Bates, roughly pushed the door open wide enough, until there was enough space for him to lean inside and shine his torch into the secluded area.

"Blood Hell," he gasped and felt shudders of revulsion sweep through him when coming face to face with a dense mass of cobwebs teaming with arachnids and grubs directly across the entire doorway. Then yelled, when hearing the shrill squeals of panic-stricken vermin racing away from the unexpected intrusion.

The foul stinking odour created by the creatures and the smell of chlorine and other chemicals sent the officer`s stomach into a nauseating spasm that doubled him up in extreme pain.

Immediately, Joan, rushed to his side offering to help him, but he brushed her off telling her he was alright and asking her to give him a minute as he slammed the door shut and leant against it. Bates, stood leant against the door, mopping his brow on his sleeve as sweat poured down his face, at the same time shining his light onto the floor hoping that none of the vermin had escaped into the space where they were now standing.

"What is it? What's in there?" Joan, asked in concern.

"Nothing, nothing of any importance," he replied shakily. "Only a load of fucking spiders and vermin, the whole area was obscured because of the density of cobwebs and filth sticking to them that stopped me from seeing anything that could have been left further inside the attic." "This area were we're standing appears to have been added at a later date, and appears to have been constructed to seal off this area from the rest of the attic. But why?" he questioned, shakily, placing his torch flat on the table and pressing a switch so that the beam spread about the entire space.

"We will find out soon enough," Anne, replied, moving over to the two levels of shelves that were fitted on one of the walls with the cupboards below. To her disappointment however, Anne, discovered that all of the cupboards she opened were empty, but when coming to the last one she found that it was locked. Puzzled, she called to her mum informing her that the end cupboard was locked and asked if she had a key that would open it.

Joan, took a number of keys from her pocket, then turned and handed them to Anne, telling her to see if anyone of them fit. She then returned to Bates, who was trying to assess what was in the jars lining the bottom shelves.

"What the hell's in these?" he asked, pointing to three large jars amongst other receptacles with strange shaped objects floating around the liquid inside.

"They look like something pickled and there's writing and dates on them," he muttered querulously, running his fingers over the discoloured glass. "There's loads of them' the shelves are full and they are all different sizes." He couldn't think of anything else to say, as he was so shocked by the bewildering sight. Then to his horror when on close examination, he realised that the items floating in the liquid appeared to human body parts.

"Oh my God!" Joan exclaimed loudly, when taking a closer look and desperately trying to hold back the tremor in her voice. "Some of these specimens are fully formed babies and unborn foetuses," she wavered, staggering back in alarm.

"Mum, there are more strange things in the jars above," Anne, called, breaking into her anguished thoughts, "they look like body parts."

CHAPTER FIFTY FOUR

THE FOETUSES

Everyone's mind was in turmoil, as they stared in disbelief at what they were seeing. Forcing herself to overcome the despicable sight, Joan moved over to her daughter's side to enable her to get a clearer view of what Anne, was pointing to on the top shelf.

"I'm too short to read it mum, but from what I can see it doesn't look very nice does it? "Standing on her tiptoes, Joan, strove to read the untidy scribble printed on a section of jars, but she couldn't quite make out what was wrote there nor what was in them.

"Officer Bates, could you come here and take a look at these? What do you think they are? I can't reach to read the writing on the labels, it is too faded?"

"Please! Bates is enough!" he responded, as he approached her and began studying the writing to identify what was in the storage jars on the top shelf. "Bloody Hell, what the devil has been going on here? He expressed angrily, as he examined the jars. "All of these components are filled with body parts: brain, liver, kidney, heart ,lungs. Somebody has been taking organs from people and preserving them in formaldehyde. As for the lower shelves, well you can see for yourself what's in those. "Joan already knew what was stored in the jars below. Amassed on the shelf, were jars of unborn foetuses and fully formed babies that had been aborted and preserved in formaldehyde. "I can't believe this," she wavered in an agonizing tone, then felt her stomach do a double take, when reading that three of the labels stated that three of the aborted babies were the foetuses taken from Matron Elliot.

CHAPTER FIFTY FIVE

THE CUPBOARD

"Mum none of these keys fit the cupboard lock," Anne, called in frustration.

Joan, however, was oblivious to what Anne, was saying. She was staring, immobilized by shock and totally devastated by what she was seeing in the jars and what was written on the labels attached to them.

"Mum?"

"Shush," Bates, whispered, placing a restraining hand on her arm and held his hand to his lips for Anne, to remain silent, as he threw an anxious glance over towards Joan. "Don`t disturb her` your mother is upset after discovering what the objects are in the jars, and who they belong to," he murmured, keeping his voice low as he took the keys from her numb, trembling hands.

"The writing on some of those labels is old and faded," he expressed and turned his attention back to the cupboard, endeavouring to open the door. But none of the keys would unlock it. Cursing, Bates, took hold of the handle and pulled, thinking it might be stuck, but the stubborn door would not budge an inch, and In frustration, he began kicking the door with his heavy duty boots, but despite his efforts it didn't even shudder or move.

"The fucking thing!" he roared in frustration, causing Joan, to stop what she was doing and glance towards him. Bates, however was furious at being unable to open the door and stamped over to the corner of the attic, wanting to be alone while he attempted to gain control of the anger and fury surging through him. It took a few moments however for him to calm down, but when he did, Bates, realised that he was standing on his own, in a pitch black corner of diminutive space of the very small room, where everything was hardly visible and his lamp was on the table at the centre of the room, that was when he felt a sliver of fear run up his back.

"Shit," he cursed and hurried over to Anne, who was still trying to work out how to open the cupboard and asked her to shine her torch into the slight gap where the bolt shoots into the lock that he had observed earlier. "The only way of getting into that cupboard is for me to prise it open with this lever," he told her, stepping back to study where to place the jemmy. "I'll have to be careful though, I don't want to cause too much damage to the wood or we could get into some bother. But if there is something concealed in that cupboard, then it's obvious that the person who put it there has something to hide, otherwise the cupboard wouldn't be locked, and I want to know the reason why, and what for?" he added grimly. "Let's ask your mother what she thinks," he said, giving Anne, an affable nudge.

"Mum," Anne, said hesitantly.

"What?"

"None of the keys fit the lock on the last cupboard and we can't get it open, so Bates, has suggested that we use the jemmy to prise it open."

"If it means finding out what has been going on at this bloody hospital then I agree," Joan, fumed. "Never mind worrying over the damage` force the bloody cupboard open. There's bound to be a document somewhere listing what every object in these jars was being kept for, and the purpose for collecting and preserving them in formaldehyde."

CHAPTER FIFTY SIX

FINDING THE DIARY

The silence in the attic was intense as the three people were too shocked to say anything after their gruesome discovery! The only sound to be heard was the wind as it howled and whistled eerily about the roof of the old building, rattling the slates and shaking the entire space they were standing in. The force of the gale as it battered the hail and sleet against the ancient building triggered alarm and fear to spread through all three of them. As they constantly scanned over their shoulders to peer into the bleak depressing shadows, half expecting someone, or something weird, to manifest itself.

"I think I`d better try and get that door open`" Bates, said, nervously glancing about the dark confining space and moved over to the cupboard, where he picked up the iron bar he had dropped earlier onto the floor and began struggling to prise the cupboard door open.

Nevertheless, regardless of the care he was taking, Bates, couldn't help but splinter the wooden edges of the cupboard. The timber was old and dry rot had already set into the fragile framework, therefore it didn't take much effort for him to lever the cupboard door open then shine his torch inside.

"Hey look what I`ve found!" he called, when finding two oil lamps already filled to the brim with oil and two boxes of matches in the partially empty cupboard, while concealed behind them at the rear of the unit was a number of enormous, bulky volumes.

`That's it, Joan murmured excitedly hurrying to his side, "I believe we have discovered what someone has been hiding all these years." "Officer Bates, can you reach inside and remove them and place them on top of the unit?" she asked.

"Of course I can," he replied, "but first I'm going to light these lamps' the extra light will come in handy and enable us to see what we are doing more clearly. Not only that, the additional light will allow us to read what's in those jars."

Bates, lit the lamps and held one inside the cupboard and was surprised to find how deep it was and how far back it reached. He then began removing the heavy items one at a time and placed them on top of the unit.

"Someone must be coming here on a regular basis," Joan, whispered softly, "there's no dust on any of the -----." She was interrupted however, by Anne's, eager voice telling her that there was a smaller book that had been pushed to the back of the bottom shelf, but she couldn't reach it.

"You're right, there is," Bates, added shining his torch and peering into the dark recess that was almost hidden by a secret partition and leant inside to remove the book. "Hold on a minute, there's another behind it," he called, as he reached inside to bring out the book.

"It looks like a diary of some sort and there's a marker inside," he exclaimed, opening it and glanced inside to see what was written on the pages. "Bloody Hell," he uttered, loudly looking towards Joan, and sending her a conveying frown. "I think we should wait until we're downstairs in your room before we read this one, come to think of it, preferably all of them," he asserted firmly, as he closed the cupboard door.

The women were curious to discover what Bates meant by saying that they needed to be in their room before they could read the diaries, and they began questioning his words.

"Please do not argue with me, I know what I am saying," he declared putting the heavy items down onto the cupboard top, then buttoned his thick, heavy duty coat about himself, while at the same time taking his gloves from his pocket to pull them over his freezing cold fingers.

"I think we should get back downstairs now, I`ve checked every corner of the cupboard and there is nothing else in there` the two lamps, the tomes and diaries are all that was inside. But I do think we should take the lamps with us, they should give us more light than the torches, and" he added.

"They will also help to show us the way back more effectively and light up any creepy ghosts that maybe floating about us!"

CHAPTER FIFTY SEVEN

THE PHANTOM SOLDIER

Nevertheless, in spite of the excitement of finding the old books, they couldn't rid themselves of the feeling that they were being scrutinized by someone who was standing nearby. "Something's not right here," Bates, muttered pulling himself upright from his bent position and he turned to face Anne, whom he thought was standing beside him. Then he felt his throat contract with fear, when instead of Anne, he saw the figure of a soldier shrouded in a dull grey light, dressed in full military uniform standing beside him.

"Oh shit," he groaned, "what the fucking hell's going on here?"

Joan, heard Bates' curses and turned, then almost collapsed with shock when seeing the mysterious apparition standing beside him, and had to lean against the cupboard for support when she felt her legs unexpectedly turning to jelly. "Good grief," she whispered, stunned by the unanticipated sighting, then for some unknown reason, Joan, was overwhelmed with confusion and didn't know what to do. "Anne," she stuttered, "help me." Anne, however couldn't answer, she was stood rigid and staring in disbelief at the soldier. For a few seconds no one moved until Joan, finally felt herself being released from the hypnotic stupor, and managed to ask, "Who are you? What do you want?" she asked desperately trying to keep the tremor from her voice.

There was no response from the man, he just stood staring expressionlessly at Bates.

"That book," she pointed to the book that Bates, was clinging onto like grim death, "will help me to solve the mystery of what has been happening here." But the soldier remained staring vacantly towards the book that Bates was holding.

"We want to help you?" she expressed in a soothing tone to the spectral figure. As if he finally understood what she was saying, the man unfastened his military coat then opened his ragged shirt revealing a gaping wound to his chest. "Oh no," she whispered sickened by the terrible sight and felt a shudder of revulsion pass through her. Nevertheless she knew that she must make contact with him, for the sake of all the patients who had suffered and died there, as he was their only chance of communicating of who he was and what had happened there.

She did notice however, when throwing a quick glance towards Anne, and Bates, that they were not going to be of any help whatsoever and eventually managed to ask the inevitable questions.

"Were you one of the shell shocked victims from the second WW." The man nodded in agreement as he drew his clothing around himself. Tired and exhausted Joan, desperately fought the demoralising nausea that was threatening to overwhelm her. "Is part of your body in one of those jars up there?" she enquired in a quivering tone. The man nodded.

By now, Joan, was fighting to hold her emotions under control, as her jaw was trembling so intensely that she felt as if her chattering teeth were about to break. "We are going to take these books and read them to find out who was operated on, and where their remains are, once we have identified them then they will be given a Christian burial," Joan, told him. "Bates hold the lamp higher, then I can show him the book." But the distressed man shook his head despondently and pointed to the ground below, identifying the area to where his corpse lay. "Oh no," she groaned, "Did they throw your remains into the well?" His face became grim when acknowledging what she was saying. He then began using telepathy to transfer his thoughts into her mind.

"I`m Allan Firth from Barnsley," he told her, "I was in the twenty fourth infantry brigade and was injured on the front lines in France and brought here." He hesitated for a moment before communicating again. "Some of the men and women who were thrown into that well were not even dead," he imparted."

"Oh my God," Joan, uttered throwing a look of despair over to Anne, and Bates, who were stood Watching, mesmerised by the unusual conversation taking place before them. Joan, forced herself to remain calm as she continued to speak with the deceased soldier. "Now that I know who you are, I should be able to find your name in one of these books," her voice quavered as she spoke and pointed to the huge volumes beside Bates.

"The police right now are excavating the well and when they have brought out and tested the DNA of all the victims, then there is a strong possibility that they will be able to identify your remains. Your relations will be informed and you will be given a proper Christian burial, and your spirit will be released from this terrible place."

The man raised his head then, with tears of gratitude flowing from his eyes. He gazed at her for a few moments before drifting silently towards the door leading into the abandoned area of the attic and floated through it.

"Holy shit," was all Bates, managed to whisper, as sheer terror engulfed him. "It`s alright, he`s gone," he heard Joan, say, "now get a hold of yourself and remember we still have more work to do."

Panic stricken, Bates, looked at her, "I never expected this," he exclaimed breathlessly, clutching the books closer to his chest. "That's me fucking finished, I`m out of this job` I didn't expect to be bloody ghost hunting when I joined the force."

"This isn`t what I would normally expect either!" Joan, shouted, ignoring his protestations, while at the same time shuddering when a sudden sense of an uneasy foreboding swept through her.

Bates turned to pick up the lamp, but never made it when he suddenly let out a piercing shriek. "Bloody hell, not again!" he yelled, backing slowly away from a woman who was dressed in a nurse`s uniform had suddenly appeared in a shimmering, incandescent light in the doorway, that glid slowly towards him. The apparition suddenly stopped moving and looked directly at Bates, then pointed towards the diary at the top of the pile of books he was holding and faded away into the shadows.

"Oh shite, I can`t stand much more of this," he moaned.

CHAPTER FIFTY EIGHT

REMOVING THE BOOKS

Although Joan, was feeling nervous after coming into contact so abruptly after the other apparition, she did her best to comfort Bates. "This isn`t what I would normally expect either," she murmured softly, placing a reassuring hand on his arm. Then hesitated for a moment when she felt a shudder of apprehension race through her, after sensing that something drastic concerning Bates, was about to happen.

"Can each of you carry the other couple of Tomes?" Bates, asked, breaking her unsettling thoughts. "I can`t carry them all, they`re too heavy, but I can manage four and the diaries, but that's it and I`m not coming back up here for the rest," he asserted firmly.

"Of course," Joan, replied, lifting one of the heavy tomes, then almost collapsed beneath its weight. "Hell`s teeth," she cursed dropping it onto the top of the other, then attempted to lift them both but slumped forward under their weight, letting them fall back onto the cupboard top.

"I can only carry one," Joan, groaned.

"Same here," Anne, replied rubbing her freezing cold hands together and stamping her feet to get warm.

"Just carry one each. Now come on let`s get moving," Bates, declared urgently, as he piled the books and diaries together. "I`ve had enough of this fucking dump to last me a lifetime," he grumbled, as he lifted the old tomes and diaries into his beefy arms. He then staggered through the open door and regardless of what could be waiting there, he crossed the balcony and made his way down the staircase, stumbling at times when his knees threatened to give way beneath the heavy weight he was carrying. But he refused to admit defeat and didn't stop until reaching the bottom of the stairs, where he sat uncaring amongst the filth and grime gasping for breath with the heavy books resting on his knees and the oil lamp beside him lighting up his grim surroundings.

Meanwhile, up in the attic, Anne, suddenly came up with a bright idea. "Why don't we take the books one at a time and slide them down the stairs, that way we won't have to carry them down, then we can push them across the landing with our feet."

Joan, shook her head and gave a sigh before speaking. "And how do you propose to do that without damaging the books when we reach the debris scatter about the floor outside?" she asked.

"Oh, I didn't think about that," Anne, replied, shrugging her shoulders. "I was only trying to save us from having to come up here again."

"Well it's a good idea," Joan commented. "But I suggest the best thing we could do, would be to use a couple of the drawers. That way, there would be less damage to the books, don't you think?"

Anne, pulled a face, "I suppose you could be right," she muttered, "you're always right. "I am right, now come on, let's get two of the drawers out and put the books in those." Together they tugged and jerked two of the drawers out of their fittings and placed the tomes inside each one. They next pushed the drawers through the door and carefully edged them down the staircase. Then, when they reached the bottom, Joan, relocked the door and gate, and without any further unexpected incidents, they slowly made their way to the bottom of the wide staircase where Bates, was sat waiting for them.

CHAPTER FIFTY NINE

THE ATTACK

"Bloody hell, I don`t know how you do it but whatever it is, I wish I had your guts," Bates, bellowed, as he struggled to avoid treading on the bones of dead creatures, that crunched beneath his compact, snow booted feet every time he trod on them. This was due to him being unable to see where he was putting his feet because of the large books he was carrying.

"Never mind that` come on, let`s get away from this ghastly place," Joan, whispered, desperate to be away from the unpleasant surroundings. Then she stopped and began tapping the light fastened to her head. "Shit, the battery is starting to go on my headlight," she groaned when it began flickering, then as it gave out, Joan, cringed when the darkness settled about her shoulders.

"Anne, hold that lamp higher will you? Then we can see where were going, and you Bates, where`s the oil lamp?" she asked sharply. "You had it with you when you left the attic?"

"Hell I forgot it when I picked the books up on the stairs, it went out so I didn't bother with it` I had my torch."

"Oh for goodness, sake," she snapped irritably. "Why didn't you say something sooner?"

"Because I was too busy worrying about the bloody books," he retorted angrily.

Joan was furious at not being able to see a hand in front of her. "Those apparitions have drawn all the power from the batteries in my torch and headlamp, and they`ve practically drained all of my energy too," she groaned rubbing her head in frustration

"Don't worry about it, mum, if the torches fail, then we've still got this lamp," Anne said, holding the lamp high in front of herself, " I would suggest however, that we should get moving we've almost reached the canteen, and I want to get back to our room and read those diaries.

"Thank God for that," Bates, said, giving a sigh of relief and getting to his feet once again. Joan, watched in fascination as he managed to grasp the torch with one hand and without any effort, he slide his other hand under the books, picked them up from the window sill and began staggering in front of them with the heavy load, while Joan, and Anne, followed, pushing the drawers with their feet through the debris scattered along the corridor.

His torch however, only lit up the defined area ahead of him, and with the storm reaching its height and the howling wind forcing draughts of cold air to sweep about them, along with the claustrophobic blackness, Bates's fears began to escalate rapidly.

I don't like this," he grumbled, turning to Anne, then felt his heart skip a beat when he brushed against a mass of swinging cobwebs, motivating spiders to drop onto his face and head. "Bloody hell!" he yelled, hopping from one foot to the other, "I hate fucking spiders! Get them off me before drop the fucking books!" he screamed, unable to brush the creepy crawlies away from himself, otherwise he would have dropped the heavy tomes he was carrying.

"Shush," Joan, whispered dashing the odious arachnids away from him, while at the same time noticing something moving up ahead. "I don't want to alarm, you but something's coming towards us."

"Oh my God," he groaned, "What do you think it is? " he asked, peering into the long dark corridor.

"I don't know, but one thing's for sure` it's heading our way," Joan remarked hesitantly.

All three paused and watched, as the weird figure drew nearer waving a lamp in front of them, making it impossible to see who it was until the entity drew closer.

"I don`t believe it, it`s the Matron` she must be searching for us," Anne gasped with shock.

"We thought you were ill," Bates, stammered, as Anne, stepped forward holding the lantern higher to ensure it was her in the murky darkness, "I don`t understand."

"No you wouldn't, you brainless, half-witted, idiot, she sneered.

"What?" he gasped surprised by her offensive comment.

"I said, you are a brainless half-witted, idiot."

Bates half turned and glanced at Joan, who was stood gaping in disbelief when hearing what the Matron was calling Bates. "Now look here," he began. But he was cut off when she began ranting and using obscene expressive vocabularies.

"It was all an act." she shouted, as she launched into spates of crude, hysterical laughter.

"My God, she`s insane," Anne, whispered softly to her mother, then drew back when seeing the axe in the Matron`s hands.

"Get back," the officer hissed, dropping the books` all but one thick diary, and taking a protective stance. "I`m no use with ghosts but crackpots like these I can handle." Bates, pushed the women behind him and began speaking softly to the deranged Matron, while at the same time steadily edging closer to her.

"Patrice, may I call you by your first name? Matron sounds so formal especially when it's a woman as attractive as you."

The Matron stopped moving and lowered the axe to her side. "That`s better," Bates, said. "Now drop the axe onto the floor, then we can go into the canteen, or better still to your quarters where we will be more comfortable and get to know one another better.

A sly idiotic grin spread across her chubby features as she held out her hand towards him. "That's better," he said holding out his arms as if he was about to embrace her. Bates however, had underestimated her devious cunning, when with one rapid movement she grabbed hold of his hand and swung the axe, almost severing the proffered appendage from his arm sending blood spraying in every direction.

Bates let out an almighty shriek of pain, but at the same time his survival instinct took over and he threw his full weight at the demented Matron, causing her to lose her balance and fall onto the filthy, pest' riddled floor. Within seconds he had her helplessly pinned down beneath his burly body, flattening and immobilizing her.

"Quick grab my cuffs, there under my coat," he croaked, "we've got to restrain her' she's crazy." Anne lifted his heavy overcoat, then his uniform jacket to unclasp the cuffs from his belt. As luck would have it the Matron had landed face down and was winded, making it easier for Anne to lock her hands behind her back, while Joan, pulled her scarf from around her neck to make a torniquet for his badly injured wrist while he sat propped against the wall groaning in pain, and unable to stand.

"Get hold of your injured hand and try to hold it in place," she yelled, " you must take the weight of it otherwise you will lose it!"

Despite the pain and bloody mess, Bates, did as Joan, instructed, then when everything was under control, she left him sitting on the floor next to Matron with Anne, trying to keep him calm, while she raced to the canteen for help.

As luck would have it, a four, nurses and a doctor were inside talking when Joan, burst in. They took one look at her ashen face and bloodstained clothing and rushed to her side, asking if she had been injured.

"I'm alright," she whispered breathlessly. "Matron has attacked us with an axe and has almost severed the officer's hand from his wrist' he is laid in the corridor and I have tried to stop the bleeding, but you must hurry before he goes into shock!"

CHAPTER SIXTY

RECORDED DETAILS

Joan, and Anne, could hardly believe what they were reading when they examined each diary and studied the tomes. Each book held a recording of the names of every person whose body parts had been removed and preserved in the jars in the attic.

Joan, however, was shocked when reading what the Matron had written in the back of one of the diary`s namely that her date of birth was July 2$^{nd}$ `1970, and that her brother Mark, who was four years older than her, had started sexually abusing her when she was only seven years old. She became pregnant by him at the age of thirteen and with the people he knew, he had managed to arrange an abortion for her. She became pregnant again by him at the age of sixteen, by then he had enrolled in the medical profession, where once again with the contacts he had, he had arranged for another abortion. The Matron was deeply in love with her brother when he made her pregnant again at the age of twenty. Even though she married Harry Peterson, she continued having sexual relations with her brother Mark.

All four of the aborted, foetuses, in the jars were hers, fathered by her own brother, along with the fully formed babies that her husband had refused to acknowledge as his. He divorced her after only seven years of marriage. Three years later she married George Elliot, who allegedly died after falling and striking his head on a rock while they were on holiday` she collected a huge insurance pay-out shortly after his untimely death. Soon after he died she was impregnated once again by her brother, however some months later, when she was out walking, she fell, and lost the baby. That too, was in a jar of formaldehyde. She had written though about how angry she had been when her brother married and had produced twin boys and a girl, this however did not stop them from getting together to this day.

CHAPTER SIXTY ONE

EPILOGUE

The Chief Superintendent and the assembled top brass were sickened after reading through the most important and urgent entries in the diaries, noting the names of people who had died there during the first and second world wars. Details of every person admitted to the hospital were entered in the four tomes.

Both the police and Hospital Committee agreed that the Matron must be confronted regarding Incest, the deaths, the bodies in the well and the specimens stored in formaldehyde in the attic.

It appeared however that earlier, before they had the opportunity to interview the Matron, an officer from the traffic division had arrived to inform her that her brother Mark, had died in a head on collision with a fuel tanker, causing his car to explode into a ball of flames. It had been impossible to rescue him, as the heat and flames were too intense and he had been burnt to death! the truck driver had also perished in the crash.

The Matron on hearing the news of her brother`s death, had gone to her quarters refusing to speak to anyone` no one had seen her leave her rooms and pick up the axe.

After the attack on Officer Bates, she had been detained by the police, where she was examined by a doctor who diagnosed her to be suffering from a complete mental breakdown and extreme schizophrenia. The Matron, Patrice Elliot was sent to a secure unit at the Bradford Mental

Hospital, where she has been detained under the mental health act, as a danger to herself and to others. She was being held in a secure unit at the asylum before being transferred to a centre for the criminally insane.

JOAN.

After a vigorous interrogation by the police, Joan, handed the head of the Hospital Committee audio visual proof of the hospital being haunted by patients from the 1st and 2WW, as well as nurses and other patients whose families had abandoned them and were forgotten. After those patients had died, their bodies had been dissected for medical purposes then thrown into the old disused well. The Matron had ensured that all unclaimed corpses were disposed of, along with some of the nurses who were believed to have left. The corpses of the nurses found in the well were only identifiable by the tags around their necks.

CHAPTER SIXTY TWO

MEDIA REPORT

Later, news reports stated that the Hospital St Mary`s at Ilkley had been closed and demolition was due to start in the near future for a new housing development of two thousand homes. Before it could be sold however it was reported that the hospital which had a bad reputation of being haunted, had been explored by two psychic investigators who had been brought in to discover the cause of the phenomena. The investigators had discovered a museum in the basement, that had supposedly been dismantled and scrapped in the mid 1990`s. Automated dummies representing patients and medical staff that were in perfect, working order were found there, along with an operating theatre.

Unmentioned in the media report was a well that the police were keeping quiet about. But of the record it made people wonder what they had found there and had not mentioned, because of the huge amount of police activity, and the whole area being cordoned off.

NEWS FLASH

The police officer who had been badly injured after an axe attack by the deranged Matron Patrice Elliot, was flown by air ambulance to St James Hospital, Leeds. Where his injured hand that was practically severed from his wrist, had undergone surgery and the hand had been successfully restored to his arm. It was additionally rumoured that some officers who were traumatised by the grotesque findings at the hospital, had suffered nervous breakdowns and were unable to carry out any further duties. Items preserved in formaldehyde had been discovered in the attic, but the police would not say what they were. The police however are now trying to contact the relatives of people missing from both the 1st and 2nd WW, and the patients from the hospital who had not had a death certificate issued. Additional investigations are to be carried out by the police and other authorities, before any further statements will be given to the press.

CHAPTER SIXTY THREE

GOING HOME

As the last of their gear was packed into the vehicle and they were safely inside, Joan turned to Anne, as she drove away from the horrendous building saying. "I`ve rung your dad to tell him that we`re coming home."

Milton Keynes UK
Ingram Content Group UK Ltd.
UKHW011956211223
434792UK00001B/4